SANDWICHED BETWEEN HOSTILE SPACESHIPS!

There were two spaceships coming up fast on the screen. They refused to budge for the "Gabby," the little craft with a secret load of gold for a distant planet. How could anyone have learned about the shipment? Would someone—from home or from far away—dare to hijack the precious cargo in the unpoliced galaxies?

One spaceship hovered behind. Was it watching the show or backing up the other two?

Gil had to make split-second decisions—or go the way his brother Ken went when he disappeared at the edge of the Cluster a year ago.

We will send you a free catalog on request. Any titles not in your local book store can be purchased by mail. Send the price of the book plus 50¢ shipping charge to Leisure Books, P.O. Box 270, Norwalk, Connecticut 06852.

Titles currently in print are available for industrial and sales promotion at reduced rates. Address inquiries to Nordon Publications, Inc., Two Park Avenue, New York, New York 10016, Attention: Premium Sales Department.

STARDRIFTER

Dale Aycock

LEISURE BOOKS   NEW YORK CITY

A LEISURE BOOK

Published by

Nordon Publications, Inc.
Two Park Avenue
New York, N.Y. 10016

1

"Corbett," Dunn's message read, "if you want the Gabby out of this damned place get your ass over here on the double!" It wasn't signed, but it had Dunn's indelible crispness of language and his Spaceworks Logo in bright green at the bottom of the yellow paper.

The message, waiting for me this morning when Beth and I got back from the beach made me briefly uneasy, but I was in no mood to take it to heart. A week with the most beautiful girl in the cluster isn't conducive to fast action of any kind.

Beth dropped into the lounge beside me. "What is it, Gil?" She had specks of sand in her hair. I brushed them out. Soon the last trace of our week would be gone down the drain. Sad that it could be washed away so easily. I kissed her and tasted sea salt. "It's nothing. Just Dunn telling me the Gabby's ready." I shoved the yellow paper into my pocket.

Beth's eyes darkened. "So soon? Does that mean you'll be leaving?"

I nodded and ran a finger across her soft cheek. "Federation willing, I'll leave soon as I can load on a cargo for the Coral Sun Systems." I sighed. The real world was closing in again.

Beth nestled closer into the curve of my arm.

"What about us?"

I looked at her, really looked at her, dark hair, green eyes, pert nose—my heart did its usual flip. The words were so close to the tip of my tongue—marry me, I wanted to say—but I was too practical. A trader with my record of disasters couldn't ask the daughter of the Marquessa of Sandyminder to marry him. Not while Corbett Trading Venture still struggled to recover from the disappearance of my brother Ken and his ship, the Arabella, eight months ago. If the Federation would ever let us collect on the insurance—of course what little spare credits I possessed had gone into the Gabby's modifications. Thinking of those modifications I became uneasy again. A picture of the Gabby flashed in my mind—long sleek lines, silver and white outer shell—according to Dunn she'd be the "fastest damned ship in the whole damned Cluster!" But was he right? We wouldn't know until . . .

Gently Beth shook me. "Where are you? All of a sudden you went blank."

I smiled around my uneasiness and kissed her again. It was easier than trying to explain.

Quintus V—the Spaceworks. Dunlevy's main shop. Racketing air-weld hammer, the metallic ring of voices yelling to get above the noise. Men running the catwalks. The acrid smell of superheated metal. Five ships suspended in 0-grav magnetic netting from the huge domed roof.

In the middle of it all, right above my head, my Class Four trading Vessel, my Gabby. Like an actress getting last minute touches before she went on stage. Uneasily my stomach knotted.

Staring up at her I couldn't see anything to be done. Her sleek lines reminded me of a racing bird. Fifty meters long, fifteen wide, built for speed, as Ken would have said, not comfort. The propulsion pods were all in place, two double circles jutting out around her nuclear core. Shielding drawn across her translucent nose.

Good. Not even an expert eye would notice the change in her tail sheathing to handle the new fuel—or would it? If Federation guessed what we were doing they'd be on us so damned fast. . .

Strong fingers gripped my arm. Guiltily I jerked away then realized it was only Dunn himself.

He glared at me. "Where the hell you been? I've looked all over Illana Port—" He broke off touching his earcaps. "Can't hear a thing. C'mon down to the office."

I hesitated. Why was he so mad? Sure, I'd been out of touch for a week but what did he care? My uneasiness deepened. Slowly I followed him down the walk and into the office.

Dunn slammed the door and pulled off his headgear. "Glad you finally decided to show up!"

"What's the rush, Dunn? You knew I'd be here today."

"Federation, that's what. I've been hunting high and low—"

"Federation?" My stomach turned over. "Did they find out what we're—who told them?"

"Nobody told them a damned thing! No, that's not the problem. At least I don't think it is."

Then what was?

"It's that new circuitry for the auxiliary pods. Kolo returned the order."

The new circuitry sheets? But they were vital! "Why?"

"They said they got a stop order on all new circuitry from Federation. Some bull story about circuitry pirating. Don't believe a damned word of it. I told

7

them—" The lines around Dunn's mouth deepened the way they always did when he was angry. "I told them if they didn't have it here by tomorrow they'd never see another order from Quintus Five!"

I stared at Dunn's tight mouth. He'd issued no idle threat. He must have a hundred thousand credits tied up in circuitry alone, most of it from Kolo Company, but he was also a man of his word. If he said it, he meant it, and they'd know that as well as I did.

Then the rest of his words sank in. "Tomorrow? Good God, Dunn that means another week—" And add to that a second week for provisioning. . .

"I tried to reach you, Gil. I tried to let you know."

Glumly I stared out the office window at the interior of the busy shop. In six days I'd expected to leave Illana for the Coral Suns, an inner system whose contract specifically stated an arrival date of six weeks from today. Even using Dunn's experimental fuel and pods I'd never make it now. And it was almost too late to subcontract, but I'd have to try. Corbett Trading Venture would have a nasty penalty to cough up if I couldn't.

Feeling a hundredweight heavier, I dropped into the chair opposite Dunn. "Why in the hell did Federation stick their noses into it?"

"Who knows? And there's something else—"

Another disaster? That should be no surprise. Since Ken's disappearance somewhere out around the Brothers, a list of our adversities would make any but an idiotic simpleton give up in despair. But then Ken'd always said I didn't have any brains.

Ken. Every time I thought of him a hard knot tightened in my stomach. Was he dead? We didn't know. The Federation wouldn't investigate, and I had no intention myself of going out there. Like I'd told Dunn, and he'd agreed, no sense in risking CTV's last ship and pilot out in the no-man's land of the cluster. But even though I'd deliberately made that decision, every time I thought of Ken I felt this tightness. As if I should be doing something, somewhere, on his behalf.

Taking his time, Dunn filled a ceramic pipe with shreds of green-brown leaf then lit it. Mesmerized, I watched until smoke finally billowed around him and he cleared his throat. Damn it, Dunn, I wanted to say, get on with it. But I knew from experience he couldn't be hurried. So I waited.

"Gil, a Federation friend of yours was out here today."

The knot in my stomach grew bigger. "I don't have any Federation friends."

"Not even Mike Pelonyi?"

Mike? I stared into Dunn's accusatory eyes. Mike and I'd been in the Federation Academy together six years ago, but even during those years we'd been at odds over the part the Federation of Inner Systems should play in regulating our lives. And more recently Mike, defending the Federation's refusal to investigate Ken's disappearance, had become the first casualty in my war with the FIS. Last I'd heard, he'd been appointed a First Officer on one of the big Fed Starships, the Hawk, or the Eagle, one of those. "What was Mike doing out here?"

"Near as I could gather, he was just poking around. Wanted to know what the Gabby was in for. What we'd done on her. I told him we stripped out all her circuitry and rewired because of some bad sheets we'd built in originally."

Icy chills ran down my back. "Did he buy it?"

"Your guess's good as mine."

"What about the pods? The fuel rods?"

"We hadn't loaded her up yet." Dunn dropped his

9

gaze to his broad, calloused hands. "Gil, I'm damned well not ready to let Federation in on this."

I knew how Dunn felt. If Federation found out about his new fuel they'd take over and Dunn would lose control of the process. It'd happened once before, when he developed a new metal alloy for shielding. Now all Federation ships carried that new alloy, and all Dunn got out of it was a transfer fee. It'd left him bitter and I didn't blame him.

He puffed at his ceramic pipe, then shot me a sharp glance. "But that's not the whole of it, Gil."

There was more? A stillness touched me, almost a presentiment.

"Yep. He wanted to know if I thought you and that Sandyminder girl were seriously—"

This was too much! I banged my fist on Dunn's desk, making the telecom jump. "How in the name of God do they justify poking into people's private lives?"

Dunn laughed sourly. "What'd he do, touch a sore spot?"

Sore spot? Maybe so. I thought of Beth and our week, our delicious, lazy week on the beach. Sure, for the first time in my life I'd actually considered family association, and if I'd been crazy enough to broach the subject, I had a hunch Beth might not have said no. But, Corbett Trading Venture's precarious position not withstanding, I had sense enough to know the ruling house of a system might object if the heiress married a —mere stardrifter.

And also, damn it, I had my pride. I wouldn't have it said I'd married her for the fortune behind her.

Dunn's smile quirked sardonically. I turned my back on him.

And FIS! What business was it of theirs whether or not our affair was so-called serious?

A feeling of urgency hit me. I had to get out of here. "All right, Dunn. How soon can I have the Gabby?"

"Six days, if the circuit comes in tomorrow."

Six days? An emptiness filled me. Six days! Well, it couldn't be helped.

"Gil—" Dunn's apologetic tone made me turn. "I'm sorry about the delay. If it makes you lose the Coral contract, I'll pay the penalty fee."

The enormity of his offer stunned me, then anger came to my rescue. Did he think I needed his charity? "No thanks," I grunted. "It's not necessary."

Dunn looked hurt, but before he could say anything more the telecom chimed. Impatiently he punched the control. "Yes?"

"Dunlevy, Pete Marston. Is Gil there?"

It was Pete, CTV's bookkeeper, and as usual he was excited about something. I could tell by his nervous hand in his wild, upright hair. I moved around behind Dunn so he could see me in the telecom. "I'm here, Pete. What's up?"

"Been looking for you, Gil. Can you come down to the office?"

"Now?" I glanced at my surface hour badge. I had to be back at Beth's for dinner at Evening Seven. But I'd given myself almost four hours to move the Gabby into parking orbit over Illana Port. If I couldn't do that, I had time to stop and see Pete, then get on over to the Convention Hall and find a subcontractor. "Sure, I guess so."

Pete's voice moved up a notch. "Well you better sure as hell make the effort!" Abruptly his face disappeared from the screen.

The office of the Corbett Trading Venture sat midway down the Illana Port Causeway on the bottom level, exactly one kil from the huge old Nathan Gorham Museum. Once upon a time pride had filled

11

me when I entered the wide front doors, but that had passed with familiarity. Besides, my office, my home, was really the Gabby, not this place. Pete did more work here than I did.

Tonight uneasy foreboding walked with me. Had the Coral run been delayed? Had someone heard something about Ken? Opposite, across the causeway, Illana's sun fell below the line of buildings and had already turned the sky blood red, etching the needle nosed ships darkly in the distance at the Port end of the street. That sky portended summer heat to come, and I'd planned to be off before then—but what did it matter what I'd planned? The Gabby wasn't ready. Period.

In the office, bright lights shone on Pete behind his broad, clean desk.

I nodded a greeting while trying to read what his face had to say. He grinned and without a word flipped something through the air. By reflex I reached up and grabbed. Newly-minted, I noted, a hexagonal, a coin like those favored by the outer systems. My foreboding deepened. I didn't need to turn it over to read the legend, but for Pete's benefit I did. Tried to sound casual. "The Brothers, huh?" I shrugged. "So what?"

"So what?" Pete grinned like the proverbial cat. "So they want us to deliver a shipment of that stuff forthwith!"

"A shipment of *gold*?" I stared at him. A shipment of gold to the Brothers? Those goddam pirates? "You're out of your head!" Pete's grin faded. "Besides," I went on, "CTV hasn't carried gold for at least five years! Too damned dangerous and you know it!"

Pete came out of his chair, grabbed a contract proposal from a neat stack and waved it at me. "Don't say no, Gil, not until you look at what they're offering! You can't turn it down!"

I didn't even look at the paper. "I can't? watch me!" If I hurried I could still get over to the hall and find another trader for the Coral run before they closed for the evening—damn Pete anyway for wasting my time with a fool thing like this! I turned back to the door.

"You damned stupid kid! Ken wouldn't have—"

Something in me snapped. I turned on Pete. "You're right, Ken wouldn't have! And where is he now? You're all the time telling me how Ken would've done it!" The angry ache inside me grew stronger. So compared with Ken, maybe I was stupid, but I wasn't the one who'd taken the 'Bella into the outer systems and disappeared doing it! "How do you know it's not the Brothers who are sitting on the Arabella right now? How do you know it isn't just a trick—"

Pete ran a nervous hand through his hair. "No, Gil, listen, it isn't like that. This is legit. I checked with Illana Central. They really do have gold coins to ship out. It's a legitimate offer. Look—"

"Bullshit." I started once more for the door.

"Gil, the commission is ten percent of sixty-six million credits. That's one hell of a lot of money. Not something CTV can afford to ignore!"

I paused with my hand on the door. Ten percent? Six million, six hundred thousand credits? Why? Why that much? I knew traders I'd trust who'd do it for five. Then I remembered the penalty we might have to pay Coral. This would—but the temptation passed quickly. No, damn it, we couldn't! Not out to the Brothers!

Then the note of warning in Pete's voice hit me. I looked at him. "What do you mean, we can't afford to turn it down? We still have the Coral contract. We'll get a little something off that, even—"

Pete dropped back into his chair and tilted it to his favorite precarious pose. "Maybe you better take a look at the books, Gil. Things are falling apart. The Gabby's been out at Quintus Five so long you're going to be lucky if you have any routes left." Looking past me, his eyes widened.

With a rush of air the door behind me flew open.

"Gil, Gil! Would you look—" Beth burst in, breathless and fiery, in her hand another yellow transmission form. "Can you imagine—"

I loved Beth, but I had to bite my tongue on an angry answer. She could have chosen a better moment to interrupt. "No, I can't. What is it?"

Beth's eyes blazed. She didn't notice my abruptness. "It came just half an hour ago. Read it! Just read it! I can't imagine—"

I did. "Edward getting impatient. Wedding awaits your arrival. Come home by summer's end or I will send Edward after you."

I read it again, but still it didn't make any sense. Whose wedding? Who was Edward? Was it a joke? "For God's sake, Beth, who's Edward?"

Beth bit her lip. Finally she gritted the words between tight jaws. "Edward Randall White. My fiancé."

A vision of our past week flashed across my mind. She certainly hadn't acted like she had a—a fiancé!

Pete's chair came forward with a bang. "Your *what*?"

Beth ignored him. "Gil, don't be mad." Her green eyes turned luminous with unshed tears.

Why not, I wanted to say—to yell—but not here. Not where Pete could listen.

"Gil, Edward's someone I've known since I was

14

two years old. Mother arranged our betrothal when I was fourteen. It—it wasn't any of my doing, and I certainly don't intend—"

But she could've told me. And her mother, the Marquessa of Sandyminder? Did she know Beth and I—was that why Federation had been poking around? God, and I'd come so close to asking her to marry me! That close, yes, to making a complete fool of myself!

Thoughts of Ken, the Brothers and gold coins slipped from my mind. "Pete—" my voice wasn't as steady as it might have been. I cleared my throat and tried again. "Pete, don't we have a bottle of brandy somewhere?"

Pete pulled open a low drawer, produced both bottle and glasses. Filled them and passed them around.

"To the future Marquessa of Sandyminder," I said, and if it sounded bitter, I didn't care.

We drank in silence. Outside the sky deepened to a purple red and the lights came on along the causeway. My thoughts matched the sky. Why hadn't she told me?

Beth put her glass to her lips but didn't taste. A slow smile curved her lips. "Gil, I have an idea."

She had an idea? Great. *Now* she had one. The brandy fire hit my empty stomach but didn't do anything to warm the lining of my soul. Why had I ever thought that a marquessa's daughter would be interested in me? Or in more than a short relationship with a guy who was nothing more than an independent trader? A stardrifter, for God's sake? Stupid fool!

"Gil, you're not listening."

"Sure I am." I reached for the bottle again.

"Gil, look at me!" She already sounded like a marquessa. I looked. She stood straight, and tall, and still had the most beautiful eyes I'd ever seen. "Gil, I could tell her I was already married."

15

"Sure you could," I said. "But she'd find out sooner or later you weren't." I swallowed the second glass of brandy fast without tasting it. When I could breathe again, I continued. "Then she'd know you lied and you'd be right back where you started."

"Or," Pete said grinning, "she'd want to meet the blushing bridegroom and then where'd you be?"

Dizzily I shook my head. "And Edward might not take that lying down." I wouldn't if I were him.

Beth made an oh-Edward-phooey sound and frowned. "Then make it no lie. Marry me."

Marry her? I stared at her until she turned pink. Marry her? Now? Right now?

Pete's grin deepened. "If he won't I will."

"Don't be funny," I snapped. My head hurt.

Beth seemed torn between apology and indignation, but indignation won. "Is it so hard to imagine, then, that we could be in love and want to get married?"

I shook my head. Weren't we in love? Yesterday I'd have bet my last credit we were, but—I shook with anger—she looked so damned innocent and beautiful —why hadn't she told me something as important as this? And if we did what she wanted—would I really feel married? Damned if I would!

Thinking suddenly of the contract proposal still on Pete's desk, I knew a strange truth. I'd—I'd rather take that damned gold to the Brothers than marry Beth like this!

"Gil," Beth's voice cut like ice through my gathering fog. "It would only have to be for as long as it takes to get to Sandyminder and back."

"That's a two month trip right there."

"Then we can marry on a six-month contract."

Somewhere in my dreams we'd spent the rest of our lives together, not just six months—or the next two. "No. No way. It's a lousy idea."

16

"Gil," Pete tilted his chair back, his voice thoughtful, "Sandy's only a week's jump from the Brothers. You couldn't ask for a better—"

I whirled around, slammed my hand down on his desk. "No!"

Pete rocked forward, quiet but furious. "Like I said, before you decide, you better take a look at the books. We've had one hell of a loss. You've got to do something before it's too late!"

"If it's a matter of money," Beth cut in, "I'll be more than happy to pay for the trip."

Open-mouthed, I spun to face her. Swallowed. She'd do *what*?

"I mean," Beth smiled with honeylike sweetness, "I'll hire you to take me to Sandyminder and pose as my husband." She touched a hand to her hour badge. "Let me know what you decide. And don't bother to come for dinner. I'm busy!"

Then, without waiting for my answer, she pushed out the door and disappeared down the causeway.

2

I stared at the empty doorway. Beth would hire me? The hell she would! Grabbing the L-T Transmission off the counter I wadded it into a ball and slammed it toward the recycler. The hell she would!

The paper ball bounced off the wall and fell to the floor. Meeting Pete's amused look, I took a deep breath. "While I'm getting the bad news, I might as well get it all. Show me the books, Pete."

Without a word Pete shoved aside a neat stack of files and from the cabinet behind pulled the bookkeeping console around and level with the top of his desk. The unit's soft hum filled the quiet office.

With fingers quicker than the eye could follow, Pete keyed our particular code onto the glass keyboard and worked his magic on the system. In seconds he pulled data from the Master Book in Illana Central Bank that I'd have taken an hour to retrieve. I stepped behind him and stared over his shoulder at the glowing screen. Numbers raced across, columns appeared. Then he hit the readout bar.

When the last figures appeared he glanced around at me. "Do you want a printout?"

For a cold, breathless second I stood transfixed by the bottom figure on the screen. The last draft I'd written to Dunn left us with a scant eight thousand credits in the Bank.

I nodded. "Let me have a sheet." A moment later I held the printout, but the figures looked no better in blue and white than they had on the screen. Eight thousand credits!

Pete avoided my eyes. "Our overhead will eat that up in less then twenty days."

I nodded again. Our overhead, not counting provisioning ran close to ten thousand a month.

Pete still didn't look at me. "Gil, we have to take that gold to the Brothers. We don't have a choice!"

Too angry to speak, I paced the office, coming finally to an abrupt halt at the double glass doors. First Dunn, then Beth—and now this! How had it happened? Why now? I faced Pete again, fighting to keep my anger under control. "Why didn't you tell me this before? What do I pay you for? You're supposed to be the expert—"

"You hold up a minute, Corbett!" Pete's chair came forward with a resounding crack. "First, you didn't tell me you wrote that draft to Dunlevy before you left. And second, how do you expect me to tell you anything when I can't even find you?" Pete rubbed his hair again, leaving it wildly disarrayed. "You don't tell a guy when you're taking off anymore, and if you ask me, that's one hell of a way to run a business!"

I clamped my mouth on an angry reply. Pete's criticism hurt, but in all honestly I had to admit it was justified. I could see that now. Obviously. I'd let myself become wrapped up in—in Beth, and when I wasn't with her I'd been out at Dunn's shop helping with the Gabby. I studied the print-out again and that cold premonition returned. Where could we go on eight thousand credits? That wasn't even enough to provision for a trip to Coral—God! Coral! I'd forgotten Coral! Why did everything have to get so damned complicated?

And with Federation hassling us—a breath of hope touched me. "Did the Commission come to a decision on the 'Bella's insurance yet?" If that would come through—

Pete shook his head. "No, and I hear FIS is pressuring them to deny."

That was nothing new. The matter would've been settled months ago if the Federation had stayed out of it. "On what grounds this time?"

"Same as the last hearing. CTV didn't file a flight plan."

"We filed with Illana Port. What more does the damned Federation want?" But I knew the answer as well as Pete. Total submission to the control of the Federation of Inner Systems. Membership in the Federation's Trader's Convention. Nothing less would ever satisfy them.

"Sure we filed with Illana Port, but Federation still says they want a specific itinerary."

"Bullshit." I shoved my hands into my pockets and paced the length of the office again.

Pete grinned slightly, then turned serious again. "Gil, would it hurt that much to join them?"

"You know damned well if we did it once we'd never be free again." Ken and I, for all our differences, had always agreed on this one point. Bow to the Federation once and file that specific flight plan and never again would we be free to go where we wanted to go or free to change our minds. It wasn't worth what protection the Service Arm of the FIS could provide. It sure as hell wasn't!

Stopping again in front of the big double doors, I stared out at the now dark sky sprinkled with a dozen close, inner-system stars. Illana Port never slept. Down at the end of the Causeway, surface ship pads lit the Illana Skyport, the passenger terminals and freight yards. Illana, though not totally central, had a reputation as the busiest port in the whole Cluster. Even the moving belts of the Causeway at our door were still crowded.

I felt the urge to go out and lose myself in that crowd, to hide from the accusing figures on the printout, from the memory of Beth.

Hire me? The hell she would!

"Gil, what about the gold?"

The gold? Uneasily I thought about that gold. Why were they willing to pay us so much? Couldn't Pete see anything odd about that offer?

Pete's chair banged forward again and I felt like telling him, for God's sake, sit still. Not that he would have. Now he'd followed my train of thought. "You know, I'll bet the outer systems are having a hard time getting reputable traders out beyond the Heteras Circle, Gil. Traders have long memories, and the 'Bella isn't the only ship that's been lost out that way. Maybe that's why they've tried us."

Maybe. And maybe not. Six ships that I knew of in the last four years had gone to the outer systems, never to be heard from again. And maybe there were even more. Although the largest, Illana Port wasn't the only trading center in the Cluster.

Nathan Gorham, a thousand years ago, didn't know what he started when he brough his disabled Explorer Class Starship to this tight-packed cluster and chose a suitable planet for deposition of his crew. Nine hundred eighty-eight crew members plus children. A cross section of the whole human race. A microcosm of the good, the bad, the brilliant and the very ordinary. Everyone alive in the Cluster today traced his ancestry back to someone on that ship—had to, in fact, before a marriage contract could be issued. Easy

21

enough to do if you stayed on your home planet—just call the Contract Commission—

But Beth and I wouldn't have to do that now, would we? Raw anger touched me. I hit out against the big glass doors and welcomed the pain. "All right, we'll take the damned gold!"

Relief filled Pete's face. He grinned. "Good! And while you're at it, why don't you give Beth a call and see how much she'll pay? Might as well make the trip worth while, and it'd damned well serve her right!"

"You're out of your head!" I yelled.

But, an hour later when we'd drained the bottle dry, it no longer seemed like such a bad idea. Like Pete said, what better cover could I ask?

Three days after our big scene in the office, Beth and I accepted each other in a simple ceremony in front of Witness Toren Glenn. It took that long to get our contracts ready. Most of the intervening time I spent in a gray daze that consisted of seventy percent hangover and thirty percent heartache. I insisted on payment from Beth of the whole amount, all thirty-four thousand credits it would take to make the trip to Sandyminder, which did nothing to help the situation. She paid off with a cold, shaking hand, and hot angry eyes. Then, after a celebration which we held for appearances only, I returned to the office. Finding a ship to take the Coral run had been no problem once I'd made it clear in the Trader's Hall that I'd give up my right to the route in addition to the regular commission. Independent Trader Tess Jordan, a friend of Ken's who owned two ships and had just bid on another, grabbed at the chance. When she came down to the office to pick up the Coral papers she offered a bit of wry advice.

"You keep your eyes open, Gilly. And if you hear

anything about Ken, you don't act on it by yourself, you understand? You bring it back here and we'll put so much pressure on the FIS they'll *have* to do something!" Tess was one of the people who refused to believe Ken was dead.

"Sure," I said and promptly forgot it. My mind was already on provisioning for our trip.

Later that same evening Dunn called to say the Gabby was ready. By working his crews around the clock he'd finished her two days ahead of schedule. That same night I moved the Gabby to her regular parking orbit above Illana's port.

The provisioning of any ship is a problem in logistics. Four weeks to Sandy, four weeks back—a three or four day side trip into the Brothers—if the Brothers representative ever decided to come across with the contract. Pete worried that he might have changed his mind, but I had this funny feeling he wouldn't. While we waited Pete saw to it that the raw materials to feed the synthesizer and clothes units were sent aboard, and I busied myself rechecking all units to make sure they were in proper working order. Beth sent a message that she'd come aboard when we were ready to leave, which suited me fine. The less I saw of her, the better.

Pete came aboard with the last of the provisions and obviously something on his mind. He fidgeted and paced and watched me check off my systems list. FInally I couldn't stand it any longer. "Okay, Pete, now what's wrong?"

He leaned against the tank gauges. Now that I'd challenged him to say what he was thinking, he seemed reluctant. "I think—"

"You think what?" I slammed the connector closed, felt the jar as it pulled back into the hull recess, then pushed him aside to final-check the capacity board.

23

All full. I made a mark on the board.

"I think—you ought to tell Beth you're carrying gold."

"Not on your life!" Was he having second thoughts? I'd laugh if I hadn't already had a few myself.

"But it's not fair to her. You're putting her life in danger. You don't know what'll happen once you get to the Brothers."

"So what? She's not going to the Brothers with me. I'll leave her at Sandy—"

"Damn it, Gil, listen—"

I grabbed his shoulder and spun him around. "No, you listen." I pointed a finger at his nose. "You listen. She doesn't need to know, and no one else needs to know. No one but you, me, Illana Central and the Brothers representative."

Pete pulled away from me, his face red. "You stupid or something? The talk's already all over the port that we've got the contract."

"Talk, yes. But no one knows for sure, and let's keep it that way, Pete. It's safer." At least I hoped it was. Because I'd developed one real fear. Except for the gold, we were travelling empty. If something happened and we did lose it, that would be the end of the Corbett Trading Venture, if not financially, then at least by reputation. Ken would've called it a stupid operation, a headlong run to disaster. He would've loaded up on trade items, and called it his insurance, but damn it, I didn't have that kind of time. Nor money.

Shortly after Pete departed he came back on the viewcom. "Gil, Mauro Balik is here with the papers. Are you coming down?"

"No. Bring him aboard."

Balik, a short man with large, cold eyes in a thin,

dark face, came aboard with Pete at Evening Six, startime, four hours after Pete's call. I'd given up on them and pulled supper from the synthesizer. After Pete completed introductions I invited them both to join me.

Balik's manner matched his eyes. "I have no time for eating, Trader Corbett. If you'll sign these papers we'll start the transfer."

I'm not normally rude, but I've dealt with people like Balik before. You exchange rudeness for rudeness, unpleasantry for unpleasantry, because it's the only thing they respect. Anything less is considered weakness.

"Mon Balik," I said, using the Brothers' own form of respectful address, "I have waited a considerable time for you. You can wait twenty minutes for me. Or take your gold coin elsewhere for delivery."

From the corner of my eye I saw Pete's face tighten, but before I had time to wonder if I'd made a mistake, Balik's eyes narrowed. "You have a reputation for being a man of discernment. I think the reputation is unearned." He made no move from the table.

Watching him, my conviction grew. There must be more to this whole matter than presented itself. Balik and the Brothers were up to something, but what? My heart almost stopped. Had they learned about the Gabby's modifications? But no, of course not! How could they? Dunn's crews were fanatically loyal to the old man. Then how could he—my mind made the leap with little effort. Ken and Arabella! Ken *was* alive! They had found about her special drive! And now they—but they were only guessing!

I pulled my wild thoughts up tight and made myself smile across the table. "You are quite possibly right," I said. "Most reputations are unearned. Pete, punch in some dinner for yourself and for Mon Balik too, if he chooses to stay."

I made dinner last the full twenty minutes. After a few attempts at polite conversation which drew only mononymic replies from the Brothers representative I gave up and put my attention to the food.

When I finally pushed my plate away and took out a ceramic pipe that was the duplicate of Dunn's, Balik leaned forward. "I presume we can now get down to business?"

"We can." I caught Pete's almost audible sigh of relief.

Balik reached into an inner coat pocket and produced a sheaf of papers wrapped in a green band. "I have here your contract—" he laid each paper on the table as he spoke, "Cargo Acceptance Form, Destination Entry Form and Visa. Also," he tapped the form on the top of the pile, "a Parking Permit. There is a charge of one thousand credits for—"

Parking Permit? Was he crazy? "No."

He looked up, feigning surprise. "What do you mean? It's standard procedure."

"For traders. I'm not coming for trade." The words popped out before I had a chance to think it through, but once they were said, I could see how they'd come out exactly right. Let them know I didn't want to come. If I was right, they'd make concessions.

Balik stared at me with those large, blank eyes. "But you are a trader. I assumed you would take advantage of the opportunity."

"No. I'm delivering freight only. I don't trade in the Brothers System. In fact, I wouldn't do this at all if I didn't have to go to Sandyminder anyway." Pete was right. It did make a good cover story.

Pete, shoving dishes into the disposer while he listened to the conversation, shot me a dirty look. I grinned at him and reached for the contract.

"Sandyminder," Balik sniffed, "is a system run by incompetent women."

I glanced up from the fine print. "I wouldn't say that. They've managed to keep you from moving in on them." I'd had a lot of Minder history from Beth in the last couple of months.

Balik grunted disdainfully. "What do they have that we could want?"

I didn't enumerate, but I could have. Sandy's wealth lay in her veins of ore, and her quantity of precious jewels. Her strength lay in a good defense system. Which the Brothers had tested, as Beth had pointed out, several times in the not so distant past.

Pete came back to the table with another cup of coffee from the synthesizer and I continued with the contract.

"Not every day a trader marries into a ruling house, either," Pete said. His voice held an edge that had been lacking previously. I put my finger on Clause 10—Payment, and glanced up. Was he mad at me again? He stared at Balik.

Balik laughed. "Not likely, if you're speaking of the Sandyminder."

Before I could tell Pete to shut up, he slammed his cup down on the table. "Captain Corbett and Beth Sandyminder were married six days ago. Hadn't you heard?"

Incredulity, astonishment and a hot, sudden anger flowed one after another over Balik's face. Then as if a screen had been drawn, those large eyes went blank again. Suddenly I felt as though I were staring at a death mask.

"Congratulations," Balik whispered, "to you and the bride, Captain."

"Thank you." I dropped my gaze to the place my finger still rested. Clause 10—Payment. And had to read it twice to make sense of it. Balik's reaction, so quick to come, and then so quickly hidden. What did it mean?

I started over again. Payment—Six million, six hundred thousand, *pay attention, Corbett, it's important!* Six million, six hundred thousand paid upon delivery. Guaranteed delivery within four weeks. Penalty of ten thousand credits for every day after that . . .

Frowning, I re-read it for the third time, then glanced up at Balik. His thin smile didn't reach his blank eyes.

I shook my head and tossed the contract to the table. "No deal. Find another delivery boy."

"I don't understand. What is the problem? It is a standard contract."

"Hardly. A ten thousand credit penalty? And four weeks? Make it five and five, and I might go for it."

"Ten is little enough to ask on sixty-six million—"

I stared at him, trying to read behind the mask. Without success. And damn it, he did have a point. Ten would be a standard amount, to a more accessible system. "Then make it a five and a ten."

His eyes grew bigger and darker. I thought I saw refusal. He could have argued. But he didn't. "Anything else?"

It'd been too easy. What was the catch? How far could I go? I tapped the contract. "And payment on delivery? Do you think I'm stupid, Mon Balik?"

Balik straightened as though I'd jabbed a finger in his back. "Are you suggesting we pre-pay you? Don't make me laugh, Captain!"

"I want," I said slowly, figuring it out as I went along, "five hundred thousand credits now, to my account here in Illana Central," that would put us back on a solid footing with Illana Port, "and six million, one hundred thousand in trust, also here on Illana."

"You sound as though you don't trust us."

28

"Not as far as I could throw my ship, Mon Balik."

Balik's gaze seemed to take me apart piece by piece. Then he glanced at his hour badge. Impatiently his mouth tightened. "All right. Can we start loading?"

It was too easy. He gave in too easy! Something was wrong, but what? I allowed a smile I didn't feel. "If you want to start loading before I sign."

Balik grabbed the contract from the table, wrote fast but with a neat scribe's hand the additions I wanted, then passed it back for my signature. I read it over, crossed out the original Clause 10, signed, and passed it on to Pete for his signature in the witness block. "Take Mon Balik into Illana Central and talk to Gordy Pittman. I'll let him know you're on your way and exactly what I want." Pete nodded and I turned back to Balik. "Are you paying in paper credits or gold coin?"

Balik shrugged. He seemed in a hurry now. "Whichever you prefer."

"Gold coin, then."

He lifted one shoulder in a miniature shrug as though to say it really didn't matter. "If I don't see you again before you leave, Captain, good luck on your journey."

I met Pete's quizzical gaze. Felt his thought. Yeah, good luck. We're going to need it!

Early next evening Beth came aboard with her crates. We'd been married by then seven days and had hardly exchanged that many words. Stepping through the flexible connector tube, Beth ignored the hand I offered. She appeared cool and remote and sounded the same. "Good evening, Gil." She handed over a small, light bag and stepped by me with a regal lift of her head that lost nothing in translation. She'd dressed in a comfortable looking travel tunic with blousey sleeves—a rich metallic green that matched her eyes—and the thought occurred to me that she'd never be satisfied with anything my shipboard clothes unit would produce. And wasn't that just too damned bad!

The shuttle mate appeared right behind her with an armful of crate. It was big and heavy and had a keyed lock. "Where does this thing go, Captain?"

The appearance of an additional crate surprised me, but it wasn't any big deal. Travelling empty we had room for anything she cared to bring. "Cargo One, Mate." I led him down the passageway to the door with the circled One, pushed the lock open for him and pointed to the corner with the steel straps. Her other crates had already been secured along the other wall. This was the last of six.

Giving the shuttle mate a ten-credit tip, I thanked him for his effort, then relocked the connector into place when he signalled his arrival at the other end.

When I finally reached the lounge, Beth stood in the middle regarding the Gabby's interior with a half smile that reminded me of nothing so much as triumph achieved. But the expression vanished the moment she became aware of my presence. Carefully she didn't look at me. "The Gabby is a silly name for a space ship."

Her tone set my nerves on édge. "Her name's Gabriella. It's an old family tradition to name the ship a female name. My father had a ship named Priscilla."

"And I'll bet he called her Prissy."

"Matter of fact, he did," I said. I struggled to keep the anger from my voice. "Care for a drink or a cup of coffee? We have a while to wait for clearance to leave Illana Port?"

"Don't I get the Grand Tour first?"

I shrugged. "If you're interested. I didn't think you cared."

Distaste settled in her eyes. "If I'm to spend the next two months on this ship, I might as well learn my way

30

around."

"Any time you want your money back—"

Beth spun away. "What's in there?" She pointed toward the glassed-in nose of the ship with its panel of controls, flight recliners and flight screen.

"Control room." Each flight control recliner was a single wrap-around unit that contained seat, hand controls for guidance, foot controls for the pods, and a view of the big screen overhead. It looked complicated, but it wasn't. "The left seat is designated First Control, and the right is Second Control."

"How original." Beth touched the large screen then brought her hand away as though the screen were dusty, which it damned well wasn't! "And this is—the lounge?" I nodded. She turned, pointed behind me at the passageway we'd just come through. "And is that the galley? Where do I sleep?"

I stepped and slid back the door of the main sleeper. "Right here." I tossed her little bag to the narrow bed. "Utility room back there," I pointed to the tiny head and enjoyed Beth's flash of dismay, "and clothes unit here." That unit combined a recycler and dispenser and fit in the small space between the door and bunk.

"Isn't there a mirror?"

I almost grinned. "Back of the locker there."

"Not very big, is it?"

I bristled at her note of criticism. "You've got the bigger of the two." I backed out and stopped in the passageway that separated the sleepers and formed the galley. "This is the galley, as you so astutely noted. Your food synthesizer is this unit on this side, and that is the recycler. Everything gets tossed into the recyclers, you know. Excess food, dishes, dirty clothes and any trash."

I thought she might balk at the clothes, but she fooled me. "Dishes?"

31

"Don't worry. They're synthetic. No bone china on this ship, but what's here is good enough for the Corbetts."

"How sad for the Corbetts." Without waiting for me to answer she moved down the passageway to the bend. "What's down here?"

"Storage here in the bulkheads, the cargo areas start there, and at the far end a decontamination tank and behind that the core chamber where we have access to the core and fuel pods."

"Can I see?"

"What for? There's nothing to see. Lot of empty space."

"If I'm going to spend—"

"I know, I know. If you're going to spend two months cooped up—"

A stillness seemed to touch her. She drew a deep breath, then faced me, one hand extended. "Gil, do we have to spend the next two months fighting?"

I ignored her hand and hardened my heart against the softness in her eyes. She'd regret this trip for the rest of her life, I'd see to that. But maybe—the thought came sharp as a slap—maybe I would too.

The comboard saved me from having to answer. "Gabby 0-19-93, this is Illana System Control."

I hurried back to the Flight Controls and punched the big screen into open. "Right-o Illana System Control. Go ahead."

"We have you on the board for departure, Captain, at twenty-even hundred hours, star time. Is that correct?"

"Yes, System Control, you have us on board right."

"Are you cleared with Illana Port, Captain?"

"Cleared with Port, System Control." Which meant that all my fees had been paid, my return visa cleared, and I was leaving no bills behind in case I didn't come back. Being a trader in this day isn't the easiest job in

32

the Cluster.

A slight smile appeared in his eyes. "Very good, Captain." Maybe he thought he was being clever. "Hope you and the bride have a quiet trip." The screen went blank.

I punched the screen control off. "Leave it to Pete to make sure the whole world knows."

"It'd not sound real if there weren't people to know about it, Gil. And we won't fool my mother if it doesn't look and sound real!"

But what about the Brothers representative, Balik? Had he been fooled? Or was I the fool?

3

I still wondered how foolish I'd been four days after crossing the Belt of Hercules, the weak astroidal belt that delineated Illana System's outer boundaries. Especially when we picked up a shadow ship on the starcomp. Since leaving Illana Port we'd followed the same path that we would've taken if we'd intended to follow the Heteras Circle, the Inner System Trading Route, but now, eleven days out, we were ready to leave that plotted course behind and head off on our own. I'd just removed the cover of the star-comp table which changed it from fixed star chart to a dimensional star field, and was sitting at the board figuring the course alteration to take us out past the Oriander, Melody and Cowper systems and into the wide open spaces of the Outer Cluster. We'd not reached a normal/max speed yet and were still burning fuel.

Beth, her green cat eyes watching my every move, stretched out in lazy comfort in a flight recliner behind me. Just knowing she was there made it that much harder to concentrate on the computations. Even though we were operating under an uneasy truce, and she'd actually laughed a time or two, when I started to enjoy her company I reminded myself of the plain hard facts. She'd hired herself a mock husband and nothing more. And if that's all I meant to her, that's all she'd get!

I'd just finished telling myself that for the twentieth time when I noticed a new speck of light on the star-comp. A ship, like us, on its way out of the denser part of the Cluster. Well, that was all right. At least they were far enough behind they wouldn't get in our way.

Pulling the straight edge of the comp-stick down from its holder over the table, I laid it over the board. The gauge gave us two minutes to course change and twenty to fuel cut-out. Pushing the stick back up and out of the way, I moved around to the other side of the board and keyed in the needed course correction. The warning light came on. With no sense of foreboding, I watched. The seconds slowly passed into minutes. On the board our direction changed and I felt it in the barely perceptible change of thrust. The speck of light changed too, and for the first time uneasiness touched me. Who were they? Where were they going?

Catching my tension Beth came to the side of the table and stared down into the star field. It was a trimensional field that worked on the same principle as a holographic viewer, and it gave the same feeling of extradimensional solidity. Dunn's new tapes also gave us a much wider range than had the Gabby's original equipment. Staring at that speck moving behind us, I was thankful for Dunn's foresight.

Beth studied the field. "What's wrong, Gil?"

"Nothing." I stared down at the speck. It might be a trading ship making an outer system run, or a Federation Starship on patrol—or someone following us.

The countdown started for the drive cut off and the readout appeared by Beth's hand. She pulled away before she realized the figures weren't actually solid.

"Oh, what's this for? Are we doing something special in—forty minutes and thirty-six seconds?"

35

"Matter of fact, yes. We're shutting down everything but the ion-drive."

"What will that do?"

Her question irritated me. Not even Beth Sandyminder could be so naive about space driving. "We stop burning fuel except for the small ion motors that'll keep us on course."

"But wouldn't we get there faster if we kept on burning fuel?"

"The faster we go the more fuel we'd burn slowing down again."

"But how do you know when—"

"For God's sake, Beth, take my word for it!"

That didn't satisfy her but short of a course in fuel engineering it was the best I could do. Biting her lip she peered down into the board again. "What's this speck of light right here?"

"Another ship."

"Is it following us?"

"I doubt it. We pick up other ships from time to time. We aren't the only travellers in the Cluster, you know."

"I never thought we were." Beth watched the field for a moment. "That's odd. The whole field moves. The whole board looks like it's a deep space chart but—" she put her hand down into the field and her hand seemed to disappear— "but nothing's really there. How does it work, Gil?"

I shrugged. The fuel thing I could have explained to her if I'd wanted to, but the board was something else again. I knew only what Dunn had explained to me in a two hour lecture once on crystals, tapes and light, but I had no words for Dunn's special brand of genius that locates a moving object in a stationary field. "All ships carry them. In all your travelling haven't you ever seen one before?"

"No, I never have." She wrinkled her nose. "This is the first time I've ever been on a ship this small." She studied the board a moment longer. "Do they know we're here?"

"Maybe." I leaned against the board and also studied the field. "Depends on how big a ship it is. Starcomp range is based on maximum speed. If that ship's large and has a high maximum speed, then of course she can see us on her star-comp."

"How big is it?"

"How should I know? If she were closer I'd put her on the screen and take a look, but at this range she wouldn't even be a speck on the most high-powered starfield." I stretched to ease the tension between my shoulders. How would I know whether that ship was a Federation Class Six, a Trader's Class Four, or even something in between? If we still had normal Class Four tapes we wouldn't even pick her up, so why worry about her now? Whatever she was, if we had to we could outrun her!

"Gil," Beth's voice softened thoughtfullly, "the Gabby isn't fast or large, so how is it she has such a wide range—"

"For God's sake Beth, I never heard anyone ask so many questions in all my life!"

Beth shut her mouth, but her thoughtfulness remained. I could've kicked myself for telling her as much as I had. She wasn't dumb. Given the right information she could make enough intelligent guesses to be a danger.

But *what* would be the Gabby's top speed? Her normal high max was a moderate one K. In an emergency I could push her to 1.5. But with the new drive—a chill of apprehension touched me. On the board Dunn's calculations were fantastic. Would the reality live up to the board's prediction? How soon would I get a chance to find out? Certainly not while Beth was with me or while we were within comp range of another ship!

Staring down at the dot of light that denoted our shadow ship another thought hit me. Was this what happened to Ken? Had someone seen by way of the star-comp just how fast the 'Bella would go? Or did Ken even have a chance to test her before—

"Gil, tell me about your brother."

Startled that she should hit so close to my thoughts, I swallowed. Somehow, in all the months we'd known each other, I'd avoided telling Beth about Ken. First because it hurt too much, and then because—well, because it was hard to sort out how I really did feel. His disappearance had given me freedom and a chance to make decisions on my own. I couldn't deny I liked both. Even if, as it seemed now, I'd been making mistakes right and left!

"Gil—"

"Ken? What about him?"

Beth flushed at my harsh tone and her green eyes turned dark. "Pete said he was older than you."

Pete and his big mouth. Moving away from the board, I dropped into first control and glanced across the panel checking gauges. "What else did Pete say?" Plenty, I could damned well bet! How Ken and I had been at each other's throats ever since I got out of the Academy and took over the Gabby. How, if I'd been doing my job in the first place, Ken never would've had to make that outer system run.

"Not much, really." Her face grew pensive. "I don't have any brothers or sister. I'll bet it was nice having someone to be close to."

Sure it was.

"How much older was he?"

I resented her speaking of him as though he were

dead. We didn't know that for sure. Besides, why did she want to know? What did she care? "Ten years. We had different mothers." I waited to see if she'd bite. She did.

"How did that happen?"

"My father had two wives." I frowned. "When one found out about the other they both left him and he had to raise us by—"

Angrily Beth tightened. "Gil Corbett, that's not true!"

"How do you know it isn't?"

Her eyes narrowed. She started to speak, then changed her mind. Turning from the table she stomped into the large sleeper. The door shut with an angry hiss.

I grinned. Served her right for getting nosy! Then I thought of Ken again and my grin disappeared.

Dunn said Ken took the Arabella to the outer systems because he wanted space to try her new pods and fuel. Making a regular trading trip out of it was only good business as far as he was concerned. But it should've been the Gabby. That was the original plan. Me and the Gabby. But because I'd taken off—but what good did it do to remember? Anyway, nine months ago Ken had filed a flight plan on behalf of CTV with Illana Port. Eight months ago he'd sent back an LT transmission on a flight change from Sandyminder. He'd decided to hit the Juno Colonies on his way home.

He'd never reached the Juno Colonies. The only outer system in that grid was the Brothers.

At first we thought it was a lining error, an error in navigation and that he'd show up eventually. But that would only happen if something went wrong with the star-comp and, like Dunn pointed out, what could go wrong there? Back when my father was lost, out beyond the huge red sun called the Eye of Apollo, computations were done by a calculation wheel and the room for human error was large. Since then comp tapes plus the shipboard computer made for 99.9 percent accuracy.

Which only left one logical conclusion. Ken had been forcibly enjoined from completing his route.

Suddenly, from the comp-board, a warning chimed. I looked at the screen. Thirty seconds to cutoff. I counted down with the readout and felt the slight vibrational change when the big thrusters stopped. Well, here we go, I thought, and shivered.

Was I making the same mistake Ken had made?

Or, a more sobering thought, would I even know until it was too late?

Our shadow ship followed us all the way to the Minder System and it matched our movements so perfectly I decided it was nothing more than an echo of ourselves on a star-comp. At least that's what I told Beth.

Then, two hours out from the Portals of Minder we picked up two ships dead ahead. Sitting at the board, chin resting on her hands, Beth was the first to discover them. Still fascinated by the trimensional effect of the star field, she'd spent hours a day just like that watching our progress. "Gil, we've picked up some more company."

I lay on a flight recliner hooked into a book reader and barely heard her around the ear plugs.

She raised her voice and said it again.

I pulled the reader off my head. "Nothing so strange about that." I'd recently found that travelling with someone else is a far cry from the peace and quiet of being alone. Beth, at times, had turned out to be an incorrigible talker. And the closer we came to Sandy the more nervous she became. And, on top of all that, I'd made a very important discovery. I loved her, goddam it, and I wanted her so bad it didn't matter how many book tapes I tried to bury myself in, or how many times I reminded myself how little she thought of me; it was the week we'd spent on the beach that I remembered most, not the fight afterwards. If I was still rude it was because that was the only way I could keep my distance! I sighed.

"Come look," she said again. "They're hardly moving at all."

I rolled off the flight recliner and came to her side. She was right. Two ships at—I keyed in a quick request for a time/speed estimate—at one KH. One hour away, if they were stationary. I requested from the comp their relative speed and projected course. The answer stunned me. We were on a collision course!

Both ships were travelling at a very slow fifty kilometers per second. More like drifting than actually moving! Waiting? For us?

I frowned again at the readout. A collision course? That was sheer stupidity! We couldn't collide. The auto-guidance hooked into the star-comp would change our direction to avoid such a collision before it got to that point, but—

A chilling thought hit me. We were within two hours, maybe a little less, of the Minder's portals of entry. The Minder was one of those systems that allowed entrance from only this one direction. If we were pushed off course at the last moment where would we end up?

Changing the enlargement on the field so that we saw a close-up of the Minder System and its three planets, I could also see the Brothers star beyond, very big and very bright. Then, down low center on the board, I picked up the minute double dots of light

41

that were the waiting ships. I keyed in for our projected path and a tense ache started at the base of my neck. We'd be forced off toward the Brothers!

Paralysis gripping me, I stared at the screen.

"Gil, what does it mean?"

I shook my head. "I don't know. Maybe someone wants to keep us from getting to Sandy."

"That's ridiculous. Why would anyone—"

The Gabby and 59.5 million other reasons, I thought. But seeing the problem didn't help! So Corbett, jeered my inner voice, what'd you suggest? I glanced at Beth, but she waited for me to say something.

Damn it, do something, Corbett, even if it's wrong!

All right. Slamming into First Control. I spun around and checked the gauge settings. Beth came to my side. "What are you doing?"

I didn't have time to answer. First we had to cut out the comp's auto control.

"Gil?"

I checked the shields. Sealed. Fuel? We were down where we should be, with little left in the pods but the retros ninety percent full. Another good reason for sticking to our course. Briefly I thought of those special drums of fuel—no time to load it, even if I wanted to.

"Gil, I insist you tell me what you intend—"

"Beth, damn it, sit down and shut up." Touching the screen panel I brought the big overhead screen to life. The star field ahead was fairly empty, but dead center was the Minder star, the brightest object in the sky but still too far away to give even the illusion of sunlight. The planet Sandyminder wasn't even visible yet on the screen.

Beth stared upward too. "Why, that's Minder. But I don't—where are the ships?"

42

"You can't see them at this distance." And probably wouldn't, anyway. Not with them between us and Minder. I frowned at the screen. Should I cut the speed? Would it give me more maneuverability—or make the Gabby only more vulnerable?

Beth turned back to the board and stared down into the star-comp's field. I reached out and fired the tiny retros and fire appeared briefly on the screen. The Gabby's speed indic fell from 1 K to .99Ks, then .98. When we reached the .80 mark I slammed off the retros. The screen returned to normal.

Nervously Beth laughed. "They're getting closer, and so is the ship that was behind us."

Damn! The ship I'd almost decided wasn't a threat! "Is it coming in fast?" Coming in for the kill?

"No—no, not now. It's beginning to slow."

Watching the show? I bet! "Okay, then forget it. Watch the other two." I flipped the power up on the screen, but still the ships ahead didn't show. I flipped it again and the two ships appeared as minute double shadows against the bright top edge of Minder.

I glanced down at the indic again. Still .80 kps. Much too fast for any fine—or was it—

"Gil, how far apart are they?"

I considered. "Five, ten kils, maybe less."

"What—what will you do?"

I wondered if I should say. Quite possibly it wouldn't work—but what other choice did I have? To go off course out here would be damned well a disaster! Beth waited. Hiding my doubt, I grinned. "What will I do? Scare the hell out of them!" And me too, probably.

Beth's lips tightened. "How? Go between them? But, Gil, that's like—trying to thread a needle!"

"Worse than that," I said. I might as well tell her the truth. "The one on the left is on our heading. If he

43

doesn't move we'll hit him."

Silence filled the space around us. Horror crept into her eyes. "You'd risk both our lives? You—you don't have the right!"

Anger boiled up in me. I didn't have the right? Who was she to tell me that? "I have the right to do anything that'll save my ship!" And damn it, I had to gamble that whoever piloted that ship dead ahead would read my message loud and clear. Get the hell out of my way because I'm coming through!

I looked up at the screen again. The eye of the needle? I shivered. Apt description! And at .80 kps, a variation of one tenth of a degree would fling us so far off course we'd not have fuel enough to try again without using Dunn's new stuff.

Unless . . .

The thought sneaked in and caught me unaware—unless I made a small enough correction to recover immediately!

"Beth—" My voice sounded loud in the quiet of the control room, "how far away are they?" I had no feeling for the passage of time.

"I—can't tell."

"What does the damned readout say?"

"Nine—eight thousand Ks—seven—"

"Has that one on the left shown any movement?"

"No."

I waited a long heartbeat, watching the screen. The black double dots grew slightly larger. *Okay, Corbett, he doesn't believe you. What now?*

Put up or shut up. That's what Ken always said. Put up—or—my jaw tightened. Slamming the control forward, I felt the jar as the Gabby's pods received the influx of fuel and spewed out the force of blue fire from her tail. The speed indic jumped from .80 to .90 and climbed back toward our original 1k. *Come on, damn it, get out of the way!*

But now I knew he wouldn't.

The approach alarm went off.

"The machine," Beth said with icy calmness, "is smarter than the man who runs it."

I couldn't reply. Instead I glanced down at our heading. If that ship lying dead in our path had moved, we'd hit the Minder Portals head on and then begin our spiral descent into Sandyminder only minutes behind schedule. But now . . .

"Gil—" The anger had fled from Beth's voice. "Do you really mean to hit him?"

Did I? I still wasn't sure. My hand tightened on the control. The speed indic touched 1K and went over. At eye level a warning light flashed. Sixty seconds
. . .

I changed the screen to hold the image of the two ships. Class Fives, larger than the Gabby—no identifying marks. And less than my guess of five kils apart. More like three right now. But the one ship, to our right, was moving away. The other, as before, seemed dead in space. No movement, no life. They were expecting us. Would the outposts see what was happening? They should, if they weren't blind! Why didn't they—but of course we were still outside their system boundaries. They wouldn't . . .

Excitement vied with dark dread. This was the kind of flying Ken accused me of. The kind kids do. Reckless. Calling for hair-trigger responses. *But you're no kid, Corbett!*

What if I wasn't fast enough?

Feeling Beth at my side I shook my head. "Get away, Beth. Sit down!" I didn't take my eyes off the closing ships.

The warning bell sounded again. Fifteen seconds! I started counting to myself—each second seemed an eternity—I couldn't take my gaze from the screen to look at the speed indic—three-one thousand two-one thousand—one—NOW! I moved the control a fraction of an arc and then back again—one-thousand!

The Class Five flashed by so big it seemed to explode on the screen and then it was gone, and we were heading directly down the safe corridor to the Portals of Minder.

Flipping the controls back to the star-comp, I fell against the seat and rubbed my sweaty face with shaking hands. *You're too old for that kind of trick, Corbett!*

"G-Gil C-Corbett," Beth stuttered, "I—h-hate you!"

4

Using Sandyminder's gigantic grav-grid, the Gabby labored to surface like an oversized bird fallen from the nest.

Sundown. Bells. Two days after our horrendous confrontation with the two strange ships and our subsequent passage through the Portals.

I chose the time on purpose hoping to ease the tension still between Beth and me, but Beth didn't seem to notice. She tightened angrily every time I tried to start a conversation.

Pressing the lock release to open the small people-port, a strange finality filled me. We approached the end of our mutual road. Somehow it made me feel very sad. "There you are, Beth. Home in time for Bells."

Brushing past me, Beth walked out and tilted her head in the wind.

At dusk the City of Sandyminder falls under an expectant hush. Activity stops. The sinking sun reflects off the golden towers that delineate the line between city and desert. A hot breeze is born in the sandy wastelands and moves inland toward the waiting towers.

The Minder star, an orange ball of fire, falls to the distant horizon and the first tall tower sends out its melodious tone under the soft stroke of the desert's breath. Then, one after another, each tower takes up the melodious chime until Sandyminder sings. It's a music heard nowhere else in the Cluster.

It made my throat ache with its beauty.

Beth listened, her face filling with such pure pleasure that I had to smile. This was the same girl who, on the beach of Illana, had told me how much she hated Sandyminder. But I didn't believe that. Not now.

Night fell too soon and the wind died in the same manner it'd been born. The singing faded away until only the last, tallest tower sang softly in a very slight breeze.

Turning to me in the dusk Beth looked lovelier than ever. "I didn't realize how much I missed it, Gil. Thank you."

I shrugged. "Don't thank me. The wind did it."

Beth might have laughed, but then, looking beyond me, she caught her breath. "Gil, look! A hovercar coming from the terminal. She's sent a car for us." She shivered.

Did Beth mean the Marquessa had sent a car? I turned and saw what Beth had seen. A cloud of dust moving toward us.

Without resistance from Beth I put my arm around her shoulders and drew her back up the ramp to the Gabby's interior. "No need to get nervous. Come on, we'll wait inside."

But once inside Beth pulled away again. Her voice held a slight tremor. "Mother will want us to stay with her this evening." She laughed. "That might prove embarrassing."

I had a vision of all that gold coin left unprotected. "I can't stay with your mother tonight."

Beth spun around, her eyes flashing a barely con-

48

tained anger. "Why not?"

I just looked at her. Whatever closeness we'd felt a moment before was gone. Her chin tilted in that autocratic way that'd become so familiar. She bit on her words. "Surely I've paid for more than just a ride to Minder and back?"

"If you think so, we can both stay on the ship."

Her voice hardened. "You're just being obstinate."

"No—" Even if I sounded like it.

"Then you're hiding something!"

Just the way she said it made me mad. I shoved my hands into my jacket pockets and stared down at her. "I'm staying here tonight. I don't give a damn whether you go or stay. Makes no difference to me."

No woman is pretty when she's angry. When Beth's mouth turned down, her features took on a sharp, hard look. "Gil Corbett, I won't be talked to that way!"

"What will you do? Throw a tantrum?"

Faster than I could blink she struck out and the sound echoed in my head like the crack of a whip.

What the hell? I stared at her.

She flushed, and caught her breath. "Oh, Gil! I'm—I'm sorry."

I rubbed my stinging cheek. "You ever do that again, Beth Corbett—" I put emphasis on the Corbett"—and I'll turn you over my knee!"

"Which," said an amused voice behind me, "is what I should have done years ago."

Beth gasped and I turned.

Facing me was one of the loveliest women I've ever seen. An older, more mature version of Beth. Obviously, the Marquessa of Sandyminder.

"I must admit," she continued as though it were an everyday occurrence that we should stand there open-mouthed, "when I heard of your marriage I was doubtful. Now I don't know whether to offer you condolences or congratulations, young man." She studied me with a severity just tinged with humor. "May I come in?"

I grinned in spite of myself. "Be my guest." As though she needed my permission.

The Marquessa nodded and swept by us with a regal lift of her head reminiscent of Beth's. "You have a charming smile. Is that why Beth married you?"

"Ma'am, I don't presume to know all the reasons Beth married me."

"Then why—"

"Mother, for heaven's sake, stop it!"

The Marquessa smiled at her daughter. "Stop what, dear? I'm merely getting acquainted." Sweeping down the length of the lounge, a whole eight meters, she studied the paneled walls, the star-comp table and viewscreen, the Simex and book tapes along one shelf. When she turned back the humor in her eyes had gained a touch of grimness. "I have a new son-in-law and you tell me I can't talk to him? Shame on you, Pundie."

Pundie? I glanced at Beth. She was bright red. She shut her mouth. Pundie? I laughed out loud.

Then suddenly I was the recipient of the Marquessa's intense and undivided attention. My laughter died. Her gaze took me apart piece by piece. Then she nodded. "I can think of several good reasons she might have married you. The question is, why did you marry her? You look like you have more sense." Before I could think of a suitable reply she changed the subject. "You two *will* come up to the hall for dinner tonight." She glanced down at a jeweled time badge on a gold chain around her neck. "At 7:30, if you please."

I felt compelled to assert myself, lest I be buried under her assurance. "No, Ma'am."

50

Coldly the Marquessa studied me. She wasn't any more used to the word than Beth. "No? Why not? You don't want to leave your ship? Commendable, no doubt, with the cargo you carry, but you can use a field seal. Perfectly safe. I'll have one sent over from the terminal. The air car will be here at 7:15. We're having a little reception in the main hall after dinner, so both of you be presentable." With a final, dismissing gesture she swept past us, down the ramp and back into the waiting car. With her abrupt departure the lounge seemed larger.

Numbly I stared after her. Her mention of the cargo—did she know about the coin?

With a near hysterical hiccup, Beth laughed. "I'm sorry, Gil. I should have warned you—" She turned away and wiped her eyes. She was crying.

"Warned me about what? I liked her."

"Most—most people do."

"Then what's the problem?"

"No problem."

I struggled to understand Beth's reaction. "Are you afraid of her?"

Moving away from me, Beth walked to the dead star-comp table. She reached down, touched first the smooth surface, then the frame. Her hand shook. "No, I'm not afraid of her. She doesn't mean any harm. It's just that we have different—objectives." Beth's eyes grew darkly unfathomable.

I watched a change come over her. Almost a hardness. "What is her objective?"

"To save the family."

"And what's yours?"

"To save the Minder System." Her words reached me so softly I thought I'd not heard her right. But then she turned and said it again, and her voice filled with an unspoken challenge.

51

I had only one more question. "Where does our marriage fit into the picture?"

"It's a long story, Gil, and you'll hate me—" Beth smiled briefly. "—but then you already do, so I can't do any more harm there, can I?" She moved to one of the flight recliners and perched on the edge, clasping her hands until her knuckles turned white. Staring at me she seemed to see something else. "We citizens of the Minder System have lived all our lives with the shadow of the Brothers hanging over us. Minder is a peaceful, nonagressive system with only one goal. To be allowed to carry on our lives undisturbed. If we have a good defense it's only because we've needed them in the pursuit of our peace. The Brothers' system wants political union with us. They're building ships—"

Or stealing them, I thought.

"—and raising a force to challenge the Federation of Inner Systems." Her eyes darkened and she took a deep breath. "But Minder is much too tempting a prize to leave behind. And, of course, Mother and her advisers know this." She shrugged and sighed. "I even know this."

Sitting back against the star-comp table, I tried to piece together what she wasn't saying as well as what she was. How did she really feel about it? Why was she so tense? Was it just my suspicious mind, or did I detect a note of calculation in her voice?

She smiled wryly. "I won't bore you with all the details, but the end result was that for an as-yet-unspecified treaty between our two systems I was promised to Edward. His father is head of the Civil Council on Brother Timothy."

"Why did you come to Illana?"

Beth dropped her gaze to her hands. "I insisted on a bit of freedom before all of this was to take place."

52

Her expression suddenly begged forgiveness. "Coming home married was the only thing I could do."

"Thanks a lot." I thought of Balik and his reaction when he found I'd married Beth. No wonder he'd been so shocked! I almost said as much to Beth, but I knew one word would lead to another, and I'd end up having to tell her about the gold. No, I thought, not yet. Then, remembering suddenly our close call outside the Portals, another thought hit me. Maybe it wasn't only the gold the Brothers were after. Maybe it was Beth, too. But then again I found myself wondering how much of her story was true, and the mere fact I could wonder gave me an uneasy feeling.

With the moons of Minder rising on cue an hour later, we rode through crowded streets toward the brightly lit buildings that housed the Marquessa and her seat of government. Our hovercar did more than justice to a Marquessa's daughter. Its obvious luxury added to my sour mood.

We'd both been silent for some time when Beth spoke. "It's funny, isn't it?"

"What is?" I couldn't see anything funny anywhere.

Beth laughed. "You. You're funny. You don't seem so impressed with all this."

I glanced around. The interior of the hovercar was a silky soft material, deep red in color. The car itself ran more smoothly and silently than lesser models in common usage on Illana. "Impressed? Beth, I'm only a poor stardrifter. Truth is, I'm speechless."

"You've never been speechless in your life."

If she only knew! I leaned against the door and looked out at the double moons, forever tied to each other by that gravitational force we now manipulated but still couldn't understand. The double moons. They reminded me of the Brothers. "Beth, why didn't the

Brothers move in on the Minder system long ago?" If what she said was true.

Beth waited for the hovercar to pause, then start up again. "I guess as long as they felt they would gain control legitimately they had no need for force."

"And now what will happen?" Somehow I couldn't see the Marquessa as one who'd give in so easily to the likes of Balik and his buddies.

Beth sank back into her corner. "I'm not sure." She sounded so forlorn I almost reached out to comfort her, but the closed expression on her face curbed my impulse. Instead I took a final look at the two moons of Minder and then we passed into the compound beneath the soaring towers of the Marquessa's hall.

At the ramp where we stopped, I offered Beth my arm, and with a regal walk that befitted our station we moved to the waiting doorway.

Were we suitably attired? Beth had taken care of that and I had no doubt we were, she in a shimmering, form-fitting full length dress, and I in Captain's dress whites that I hadn't requested from the clothes unit in over three years. I was a little surprised the measurements still fit.

Did we appear suitably married? Looking at the small gold band on Beth's hand I certainly hoped so.

At the door an old gentleman bowed to us, then led us inward. It was his manner, I decided, and not the uniform which labelled him Majordomo. He wore a green and silver tunic which matched the colors the Marquessa had worn earlier.

Beth's hand tightened on my arm. I smiled down at her and enjoyed the pretend feeling that she needed me.

The short hall ended at another set of wide doors almost hidden in mirrors. Impressive. The doors opened before us without the help of human hands and we walked into a room containing a dozen people or more. Both men and women were present, most nearer to the Marquessa's age than ours. Beth gazed around and I could feel her surprise. I glanced at backs and half-averted faces but couldn't see the cause. The dress was so ornate I felt conservative by comparison.

Beth's mother saw us. She flowed forward. "Beth love, and Gil. You are prompt. Thank you."

Although Beth smiled I could feel her anger. It was in the lift of her chin, the tightness of her hand on my arm. "Really, Mother, I thought this was a dinner, not a political convention!"

The Marquessa only smiled, then turned to me. "Come in, Gil dear, I have some friends I want you to meet." She swept me into the nearest group with Beth, ready to explode, trailing in our wake.

The Marquessa ignored her. "Filemon, Letsinger, Conroy, this is Gil Corbett. Beth's new husband, you know."

Sandyminder isn't kind to her men. I'd read that someplace and now I could believe it. Each man, in his own way, acknowledged the introduction: a bow, slight smile, a nod. But what each might think was hidden behind a weathered face, half-closed eyes and a guarded expression.

Skipping the women in the group, the Marquessa went on to the next three men. "And this is Mandel, Falkner and White."

Any relation to Edward? Not likely. White was an old man, and unsmiling. Of them all he was the only one I could read. He looked at me with fear.

But what did this old man have to fear from me? What would any of them have to fear from me? I meant them no harm!

The Marquessa didn't allow me to dwell on the question. She'd gone on- to naming the women.

"Louisa, Mara, Karin—" They came too fast and I lost track but received the impression that each woman belonged to one of the men. When the introductions were completed and acknowledged, and Beth had regained possession of my arm, dinner was called. After the wine and appetizers the Marquessa once again took charge of the conversation.

"Ladies and gentlemen!" Her clear, brittle tone brought instant silence to the long table. "I thank you all for coming." She didn't need to raise her voice. A whisper would have been heard as well. "I know this was quite short notice for most of you. As you all are aware, this dinner is much more in the nature of a council of war, but there was really no other way of getting you all together without raising questions in the wrong minds."

And in the not so wrong, I thought, my own included. Beth's eyes glittered with anger.

"We have with us tonight," the Marquessa continued, "my daughter, Beth, whom you all know, and Gilliam Corbett, whom you have just met. The truth of the matter is, no matter how much it hurts to say, if Captain Corbett weren't here, this meeting would not be necessary."

I glanced at Beth who dropped her gaze to her plate and then at the others. Nods of agreement bobbed around the table and almost all eyes turned in my direction. None of them was friendly.

After a pause in which I received the impression I should have felt intimidated, the Marquessa went on. "Gil dear, to say you are being used by my daughter is hardly an understatement. She wanted to create a situation where we would have to take immediate action and she did. We have had to cut off all contact with the Brothers. Our system boundaries are no longer safe."

"That's not true!" Beth sounded so much like her

mother that it startled me. Except that Beth was more passionate. "You," she gestured at the table, "all of you are pushing the Minder System into a war which is completely and totally unnecessary. Peace between the two systems is possible, but not a peace bought by a marriage of convenience!" She glanced at me. "That's why I went to Illana, and why I will return there when Gil leaves."

Oh? From one marriage of convenience to another marriage of convenience. How neat. For Beth.

A long silence followed her outburst. I certainly couldn't have said what I was thinking, and maybe the others couldn't either. For the first time the Marquessa's face showed signs of inner turmoil.

A glass accidentally clinked against a dish. The sound aroused the Marquessa and she cast me an almost contemptuous look. "Are you so sure Gil is going back to Illana when he leaves here?"

"Ma'am," I said quickly, "no matter where we go when we leave, you'll always be welcome in our home on Illana. I'm sure neither Beth nor I would have it any other way."

Beth's mouth curved into a lovely smile, and her gaze, before she dropped it demurely to her plate, held an infinity of devotion.

Frowning her unhappiness, the Marquessa ordered the first course.

5

"Gil, you were perfect. Absolutely perfect."

In the hovercar going back through deserted streets to where the Gabby lay, the only trading vessel at rest on the great gravity grid, Beth and I huddled together.

The double moons of Minder had just sunk below the horizon and their place had been taken by the Brother's star, the brightest in Minder's sparse heaven.

The evening had been long, and I was so tired it was too much effort to speak. No one at dinner had mentioned Beth's intended, Edward Randall White, for which I was more than grateful, but the people had been interested in FIS and the new educational opportunities and the opening up of a new system for colonization. The same things people everywhere wanted to talk about. They wanted to know if FIS was ready to extend its patrol on a regular basis. I had to admit I knew nothing about such matters and then the conversation drifted to trading opportunities within the outer systems. Beth had played the blushing bride with the ladies and it'd all gone off quite well, considering it was all a sham.

In no mood now to match Beth's liveliness, I grunted. "Perfect? You weren't so bad yourself, Mrs. Corbett. I almost believed some of those things you said."

Beth snuggled closer. "Oh, Gil, don't you love me? At least a little?"

I looked down at her. She was still the most beautiful girl in the universe. All my stern resolutions vanished quicker than I could blink. "Not a little, Beth. A lot." Somehow confessing that only made me feel worse.

"Then kiss me and let's make this marriage real."

Maybe it was the late hour. Or too much Minder wine. I didn't care. I encircled her, kissed her. And with her body soft in my arms, responsive to my hands, somehow I was no longer tired.

The hovercar stopped beside my dark and quiet Gabriella a few minutes later and we stepped out into the crisp chill night. Intoxicated by the feel of Beth at my side, my mind wasn't on the ship, but it should've been.

We reached the ramp before the wrongness hit me.

I let go of Beth and stood perfectly still. *The field seal*! It was—why hadn't it—didn't I set it before we left?

"What's wrong, Gil?"

"Hush." I pulled the small seal control from my pocket. A seal on a ship as large as the Gabby is generated from within, set tonally, and can only be released, supposedly, by the unit that sets it. Of course there were ways to break the seal, but most were too complicated to be accomplished in a few hours. But *this*—this damned seal could've been fixed before I got it. After all, it'd come from the Marquessa of Sandyminder. Anything was possible.

In the dark Beth's face was a white, questioning blur. "Gil, for heaven's sake, will you tell me—"

"Shut up and stay here." I jumped down off the ramp and ran down the length of the ship. The Gabby was monstrous, unnatural, lying on the grassy field that was Minder's terminal. Built for space, she looked grotesque, unwieldy, laid against the planet's surface. Why in the hell hadn't I kept her up above the atmosphere where she belonged? Was the fun of experiencing the gravity-grid worth it?

Running back toward her tail, toward her propulsion pods, I counted off the sections. Galley, storage, Cargoes One, Two and Three, Corgen and fuel pods. In the faint reflection from the City of Towers I saw nothing wrong.

Coming around the tail, I started up the shadow side. Here the shadows seemed unusually deep and the surface struts looked like white wire against the dark black grass. Still I saw nothing unusual. Coming up on the nose section I started to smile at my fears. Then I saw the hole.

Damn it all to hell!

Waist high and still hot as fire, the hole was big enough to put a fist through. I sank to one knee and tried to gauge what was directly opposite on the inside. Control panel wiring? Star-comp banks? The metal glowed faintly from the heat. How deep was it? How much damage? I needed some light.

Starting to rise, I stopped abruptly. I'd heard nothing, but I felt—a sense of presence. Who? Beth?

About to call her name, I heard a soft rush of air; pain and light exploded in my head. I fell full length, my ears ringing.

"Is he dead?" someone whispered.

"Hell, no," came the soft answer. "We should have that kind of luck. Grab that digger and let's get out of here."

A soft scramble of footsteps in the turf faded away.

I stifled a groan and tried to get up but failed. God, did my head hurt!

Beth held the heavy construction light while I, on my knees, used a pair of insulated tight suit gloves to probe the depths of the hole in the Gabby's nose. It'd taken me a few minutes to recover enough to call Beth, and even now my head throbbed in time to my angry beating heart. But the Gabby—she was my main concern. What if—? I reached into the hole. What if they'd gone all the way through? What if they'd damaged a control? What if—panic grabbed me—what if we were stuck here with the gold and couldn't get off the ground?

Hold up there, Corbett! Forget the what-ifs! Panic wouldn't repair the hole—

Wiping my sweaty face on the sleeve of my dirty dress white jacket, I motioned to Beth. "Hold that thing a little more to the right."

She pushed the con-light over and I touched the first layer. It was hot and soft. The highly reflective outer skin. "We'll need a titallium patch." I reached in further, and noted, "a ganosite, too." A laser had done this job. Probably a little mining unit. Maybe the same thing I'd been hit with. Hand held from directly below. It'd gone through the ganosite and—damned bulky gloves anyway—

"Is it repairable?" Beth sounded scared.

I worked my way around a ground strut and angled in on the hole. "I don't know yet. Can you bring the light in any closer?"

She moved the con-light in and her face in its reflected glow was flooded with apprehension. "Who'd do this, Gil? Why? Just to keep us here?"

I didn't answer. I'd already asked myself the questions and come up with nothing but more questions. Like, what would've happened to us the minute we were released from Minder's grav field if I hadn't discovered the hole?

Impatient with the bulky gloves, I stripped them off and reached back into the damaged area. The metal still burned to touch, but the heat was dissipating fast. The hole in the third layer, the four centimeter mica-menium insulation, was only large enough for two fingers. Then I felt the tight mesh underneath. It was intact. Relief filled me with a touch of idiocy and I laughed. They hadn't had time to go all the way through! The rest I could fix. "Okay, Beth, cut the light."

"Well?" She began to sound like her usual self. The Beth who would someday be Marquessa. If she lived that long.

I took the light and scooped the gloves from the ground. "Let's go on in."

She waited until we were inside but her anger built. "Well?" she repeated.

"Well, it'll take me about three hours to fix her after we leave the surface. We interrupted them before their job was done."

"Can't you fix it on the ground?"

I shook my head.

"But why not? I should think—"

"I could but I won't. Because it'd take me twice as long on the ground, and because the torch I have isn't made to work under atmospheric pressure." And the truth was, the sooner I got off Sandyminder the better I'd feel.

Taking the equipment I went back through the galley to the storage passageway. Beth followed.

Outside the Cargo One door another thought hit me. The gold: had those bastards found the gold? Shoving the con-light into its compartment I spun back to the Cargo door. If they could break a field seal, my Class Four door seals wouldn't present much of a problem. My only hope lay in how well concealed it was.

"Gil," Beth stomped her foot. "Answer me!"

I stared at her. Had she asked a question? We faced each other like pugnacious kids, all thoughts of our few close moments in the hovercar forever past. Then suddenly it hit me. She'd never been afraid of anything or anyone in her life! "Sure, but you won't like it."

"I don't—what won't I like?"

"Someone tried to kill us, Beth."

"Oh, don't be—but—that's ridiculous!"

I opened the cargo door by putting my hand on the ID plate. With a hiss it swung inward. "You think so?" I don't know what I expected, but I wasn't surprised. I really wasn't. Cargo One was a shambles. Every crate Beth had sent aboard while we were still on Illana had been ripped apart. Every conceivable hiding place torn open. Of course. It made sense. All they needed was time and we'd given them plenty.

I stood aside and let Beth step through the door.

She took a long moment to react. "Gil—this is pure madness!" She walked into the middle of the twelve by twenty meter hold and turned around. "What—what happened?"

"I'd say someone was looking for something, wouldn't you?" The floor grids were still solid. I grinned my relief. They'd looked, but they hadn't found it!

"What were they looking for?" She raised her hand to the hour badge hanging on a chain around her neck, and for the first time I noticed the small key that hung there too. Her eyes were veiled, watchful.

"Like," I said, "where I hid 59.4 mil in gold coin."

Her mouth fell open. Either she was a damned good actress or I'd really surprised her. Then another dread flooded me. The fuel! Had then gotten into Dunlevy's fuel rods? If they had—if the drums were gone—! Pushing through the mess I raced through empty Cargo Two and across to Number Three.

Checking the meter above that door my heart returned to normal. The rad level read minimum blue. If anyone had opened the door it'd be in the red zone. Leaving the door intact, I went back to Beth. "The fuel drums are okay."

"Gil Corbett, what are you talking about?"

"Fuel drums."

"Gold coin!"

"Now Beth, it's nothing to get excited about."

"Nothing to—Gil, how could you?"

"Same way you could talk me into marrying you, Beth."

She brushed that off with a wave of her hand. "And who is it for? Certainly not Sandyminder."

I just looked at her, waiting for the obvious answer to dawn.

It did, finally, and her whole body tensed. I thought she would swing on me again, and, by God, I was just in the mood to swing back.

But she turned away, her voice muffled. "Why?"

Before I tried to explain I led her out of the Cargo door into the passageway and down to the lounge. "You want a drink? I think I need one." Not that I really did. I just needed to buy time to think. How much did she already know? How much could I tell her?

"A drink is no answer, Gil." But she took the one I poured for her and sat sipping while I checked the field around the ship.

"Will you tell me why or are you just going to putter around all night?"

"Why what?"

"Why you are taking that much gold to the

Brothers?"

Her naiveté irritated me. "Haven't you ever heard of the profit motive?"

"For you? You never struck me as being inordinately fond of money!"

"We have to make money to exist, Beth. Food and fuel only come with credits!" It sounded pompous to say it like that, but I wouldn't be surprised if she'd never wondered where food and fuel came from.

"You seem to be solvent." She saw me staring at her, flushed and looked away. "Well, you didn't think I would fall in love with someone and not find out about him, did you?"

I smiled at her over the rim of my glass. "You and your mother have a lot in common. I'm sure she's also investigated my financial status." And probably knew more about it than Beth did.

"That's not nice, Gil. It wasn't your financial status I was interested in. It was your reputation. That's why I can't understand your dealing with the Brothers."

"Beth, how long have you known me?"

She looked down at her full glass. "Five months."

"Six months," I corrected. "Almost seven. And did you know that two months before we met, CTV lost a ship worth twenty-five million credits? And her pilot, my brother Ken?"

"Of course I'd heard about it. Pete—"

"Did you also know they disappeared someplace between Minder and the Brothers?"

Beth looked up. I'd surprised her again. Somehow that made me feel better. "It's a fact," I went on, "that Ken and the 'Bella were on Sandy the week before he disappeared."

"The week before? Then you heard from him after he left here?"

I nodded. "An LT transmission with a change of

65

flight plans. Ken plotted his own paths. He'd decided to swing around and hit the Juno Colonies before he came home."

"But the colonies are almost two weeks from here!"

"That's right. When he left here Ken's ETA for Juno was 12 days. Four days later we got another LT and he was right on schedule. We never heard from him again."

"And you think the Brothers—" Her mouth tightened. "Is that why you—"

"Came? No. I'm just telling you why I was so careful. I need the money damned bad, but not so bad I'm taking any needless risks."

"But what about your brother?"

"What about him?"

"Were you looking for him?"

"No." I could see she didn't believe me, but I couldn't help it. "Look, all I want is to deliver the damned gold and go home. You can stay here—"

"But if they stole it—" Confusion filled her eyes.

"They didn't."

"But that—"

"Don't worry." I grinned. "They didn't find it. It's safe. Now like I said, you stay here—"

Beth's jaw set stubbornly. "I'm not staying on Sandy."

"I don't care where you stay, but you damned well arent't coming with me!"

Beth smiled a sweet, lethal smile. "Do you always swear when you get mad?"

I clamped a lid on my anger. Beth wasn't prodding me into another fight! No way!

She waited, but when I didn't react she shrugged. "It looks like we deserve each other, doesn't it? You weren't telling me the truth, and I wasn't—"

I nodded. "And I'll bet your mother knew it all the time."

Beth's glance sharpened. "Why do you say that?"

"Only that she knew what we carried when she walked in this evening. Remember when she told me I could have a field seal to protect what I had on board?"

Beth stood abruptly. "Then that dinner she called a council of war was all a sham?"

"Was it? You know her better than I do."

"Well, I'm finding out!" Beth headed for the main sleeper and I reached for the bottle. Shortly after she reappeared dressed for the night air.

I toasted her. "Enjoy yourself and don't get lost."

"You're not funny!"

Alone I reset the field, sat down at the star-comp and pulled a star overlay from the rack below. Ken's course, plotted out to the last moment we knew of him. Would he have changed his mind and gone to the Brothers on his own? Had he crashed or was he pirated? In light of Balik's strange concessions at the start of this trip, I had to figure Ken'd been pirated, and that Balik had the same in store for me.

Maybe—the thought was distasteful, but I had to admit—maybe it would have been better to file that damned flight plan with FIS. Maybe I should have signed the Trader's Convention.

I slammed the chart away. Damn it, *no!*. I'd do it on my own. To hell with asking Federation for any help. They'd not blackmail me into signing the Convention! No way!

And if I found out anything about Ken?

Bleakly I stared at my half full glass.

Ken was on his own. Just like me.

6

I jerked awake to the sound of the field alarm. I'd been asleep at the star-comp and every bone in my body ached, along with my throbbing cheek. The steady wail of the alarm indicated someone caught in the field. Good, I thought, let 'em stay that way.

My hour badge said I'd been asleep almost three hours and we were still two hours from dawn. I pulled myself to my feet.

Using the screen, I checked the intrusion and found two people had approached the ramp. Caught in the seal they couldn't move. One was Beth, the other a stranger.

I opened up for them.

The fellow who followed Beth in was on the young side of twenty. While Beth introduced us, he studied me with disapproval and I returned the favor.

"Des, this is my husband, Gil Corbett. Gil, Des Filemon. You met his parents at the dinner this evening."

I did remember Filemon, the father. He'd been the tall, silent man with hooded eyes, the first one Beth's mother had introduced. Des looked like his father except that he'd not yet lost the youthful baby fat around his jaws. Nor acquired the hooded eye. I nodded. Offered them coffee, brandy, then considering Des's age, milk.

He flushed. "Nothing." His voice was surprisingly deep.

Beth chose coffee. "I brought Des back because he saw your brother when he was here."

"Oh?" A prickly sensation ran down my arms. But what did I care if Des had seen Ken. No one had ever denied he was here! It was after he left that . . . I glanced at Beth. She was waiting for me to be pleased. I forced a smile. "Great. I imagine he was quite busy."

"Sure. But you traders usually stick to the buyer types." Contempt for the marketplace clouded Filemon's voice.

"And didn't Ken?"

"Mostly. He went to three trader conferences, picked up a hundred-weight in Minder's gem ore, and bought twenty-five bolts of metallic lame from the mills out at Terry. He was here six and a half days."

Mentally my jaw dropped. Ken himself couldn't give me a much fuller account of what he'd done here. But how did this kid know all that?

I would've asked, but Beth seemed to read my mind. "We have a very good organization in this system. It keeps track of strangers."

And even people who weren't? What a telling point about the Minder mentality, I thought.

"It's as much for their protection as for ours," Des added defensively.

I remembered a story I'd heard of Minder's distant past, how they'd obtained workers for their mines. But that was two hundred years ago, and the mines had mechanized as fast as the traders could bring the machinery. I shook my head. Why did Minder still think this was necessary? Uneasily my thoughts returned to Ken. Was I blaming the wrong system for his disappearance? "Did my brother do anything 'unusual' while he was here?"

Hesitating, Des glanced at Beth for guidance.

She frowned at him. "Well, did he?"

"What would you consider unusual?"

"Did he see anyone besides traders?" I said.

A shadow crossed the young man's eyes. "He called on the Marquessa." He thought a moment. "And then there was that Silvernight guy. He came and visited your brother one day."

Lados Silvernight? The fuel expert? A hard knot settled in my stomach. What in the hell was Silvernight doing here? Last I heard he was teaching at the Federation University on Illana! I glanced at Beth, but from her puzzled expression I knew the name meant nothing to her.

I frowned down at my cup. "Has Silvernight been here long?"

"He's not here now. He came in the day after Trader Corbett and left two days later."

Where did he go, I wondered, but before I could ask, Beth spoke. "Des, this Silvernight. What did he do while he was here?"

"Went around to the junior schools recruiting for that experimental science school on Brother Timothy. Without the Marquessa's permission. When she found out, he got the boot." Momentarily, grudging admiration lit his eyes.

No, Minder wasn't the friendliest place in space. Then my mind slid back to Silvernight. From what I knew of him, he wasn't a rabble-rouser by any stretch of the imagination. His only problem seemed to be that he was an idealist who'd been born into the wrong century. At least that was his reputation.

But, damn it, given his specialty he could only have one possible connection with Ken. And that was the

'Bella's fuel!

Had he in some way learned about the ship's modifications? Would Ken have told him? Of course not! No more than Dunn would've himself!

Filemon stood. "Beth, if you don't need me any more I've got to get back. I'm on duty at the terminal in an hour."

Beth smiled and touched his hand. "Thanks for coming with me, Des. I—we appreciate your help."

The kid gave Beth a worshipping smile and they touched cheeks in the Minder manner of good friends.

Even though I really did appreciate the news of Ken, I resented Des Filemon's familiarity with Beth, a resentment which turned quickly into anger.

After the kid was gone and the field re-established, Beth poured herself more coffee from the synthesizer and sat down beside me. "What does it all mean, Gil?"

"I have no idea."

Beth gave me a quick, searching look. "Is something wrong?"

Pushing aside my anger, I shook my head. Besides, what did I have to be angry about? We weren't really married. Not in the heart, which is the only place that matters. Leaning my head back, I closed my eyes and tried to think instead about Ken. It was puzzling that he'd seen Silvernight.

Beth seemed to pick up on my thought. "Gil, who is Silvernight?"

I told her what I knew of the strange little man. How he'd come to prominence in the race for a better fuel. A brilliant, one-track mind. Where Dunlevy was interested not only in fuels, but in building better ships, and other things as well, Silvernight concentrated on only the one specialty. A better, faster fuel. Dunlevy called him crazy. The rest of the Cluster only

71

called him eccentric.

When I finished, Beth digested the information in silence. I watched her face, an expressive, well-molded face that hadn't yet reached its maturity. Odd that I'd never noticed that before. She and her friend Des.

Abruptly I stood. "Why don't you get some sleep and I'll go clean up Cargo One. I'll wake you when we get someone out here for your crates."

At dawn, when Minder's terminal woke to a new, warm day, I arranged with the Port officials to have Beth's crates removed. If I could've done it earlier I'd have awakened Beth and told her to get off the ship so I could leave, but Minder officialdom couldn't be hurried. No officialdom can. That's one of the first things I learned as a trader. You move at the speed of whatever system you're in and they're all different but slow.

A terminal crew and Port Master arrived shortly after I sent over my request, and when I expressed surprise at the presence of the Port Master, he abruptly produced a removal permit and a search order. "Do you have a bill of lading on these crates, Trader?"

Patience and cooperation, the trader's watchwords. "These crates aren't trading merchandise. As far as I know they're all gifts for the Marquessa from her daughter. But if you want to take a look, I'll help you open them." I thought my disarming cooperation might make him say forget it, but he was an untrustful soul. We opened each crate that I'd so carefully closed just an hour before, and he examined each item. Beth had brought her mother bone china dishes from Candulus, a set of small titalium-coated metal statues, point of origin the Dank system, and tri-panel mirrors of the kind you see all over Illana. A long rectangular box contained a tapestry-type rug. A much smaller one held a machine for measuring weights. Everything but the mirrors, I knew from experience, was quite expensive, and I wondered just how much money Beth had at her disposal. Maybe a hell of a lot more than I'd thought!

The last crate, as tall as my shoulders and twice as broad, was the last one the shuttle mate had brought on board before we left Illana. Bound together with magnetic tape bands that were locked, it was the only crate that hadn't been ripped apart by our middle of the night visitors. With the Port Master examining the lock, I wondered where I'd find the key so he could look inside, but then I remembered Beth and the involuntary movement of hand to key when she first saw the torn-up crates. Was that the right key? It was worth a try.

I went into the main sleeper but Beth still looked so dead tired I decided not to disturb her. Carefully I removed the key from her hour badge chain. She stirred and murmured something indistinguishable but then settled down again. I tiptoed out.

Back in Cargo One the Port Master and I took the crate apart; but even then we didn't know what we had.

Except that it was real wood. I could tell. I was raised on Illana, which is wooded. I've even carried real wood. It has a special feel that the synthetic never quite captures.

But this piece, egg-shaped and almost black, was only wood and nothing more. It had no seams, no esthetic value beyond what I could see or feel. Finished and polished to a high gloss, to my touch it felt warm and smooth, the way wood does.

"What is it?" The Port Master's pen hesitated over the slate. I confessed my ignorance. He motioned one of his men to turn it over. It rolled over on the floor grids and came back to an upright position.

An amusing surprise! I laughed.

"Hell, how did it do that?"

"See," I said, "it's the way it's weighted."

"But hell!" The Port Master wasn't amused. "I have to call it something!"

"Call it," I said, searching my reservoir of trivia, "a mahogany sculptured ovoid, 'Beginning of Man.'"

Suspiciously the Port Master eyed me. "What does that mean?"

"It's a wooden egg."

For a moment I thought he'd laugh, but he resisted the temptation. Stabbing the pen to the slate he made a notation. When he looked up again his eyes were hard. "What about the rest of your cargo, now?"

I smiled, hiding a sharp attack of uneasiness. "Hey, look, I'm empty. I don't have another blessed thing." But the gold, and I damned well wouldn't show that to him and have him find out I had smuggler capabilities! I might want to come back here some day!

"That right?" He stalked to the Cargo Two door. "What's in here?"

"More cargo space." As if he didn't know.

"Open up and let's see."

I shrugged, walked over and gave the lock a spin.

Each of the Gabby's cargo holds served a different purpose. Cargo Two was cushioned and sprung. I've carried delicate spun glass in there without breaking a thread. But of course it was empty now.

The Port Master seemed disappointed. "Okay, let's have a look at your Number three."

Within me an irrational anger stirred. "It might help if you told me what you were looking for."

"Trader Corbett," he said, "it's too early in the

morning for games."

"Exactly," I agreed. "So why the hell can't you tell me what you think I'm hiding?"

"We've been told you're smuggling gold!" The Port Master watched my jaw drop and shook his head. "And I don't care who you are, or who you got on board, when we catch a rumor like that, we have to check it out."

A feather chill touched me. Who'd done this? The Marquessa? I shuddered, thinking how closely he'd scrutinized the wooden egg. If he'd lowered his examination to the grid beneath his feet . . . "Yes,' I nodded. "I can understand that you have to check." I walked across the spring floor to the Cargo Three door and touched the small, multi-layered window. "There's drums of extra fuel. You'll need a white-suit to go in there. Would you like help?"

I was stripping off my damp white-suit forty-five minutes later when Beth appeared in the door of my sleeper. "What's all the noise about?" She was still half asleep and had made no protest at all when the Port Master had sent men in to search around her. But the feel of the rough-running corgen had brought her out. "What are you all dressed up for?"

Having just said goodbye to the very doubting Port Master, who'd found nothing to corroborate his rumors, I was in no mood for another interrogation. "We just had an inspection."

"Why?" Her eyes began to focus and she looked more alert.

"They thought I was trying to smuggle gold." I kicked off the wet boots and stepped out of the suit. "I sent those crates over to your mother's." I dug out the key for her, "Here. We had to open up that crate."

She looked suddenly apprehensive. "What did you

do that for?"

"Open it? Because the man told me to."

"No, I mean send them over—"

"Because, damn it, that's where you told me they were supposed to go." I rolled up the suit and grabbed a glance at my sore cheek. It was red and puffy where I'd been hit, but it looked much better. I checked my hour badge. "It's half an hour to lift-off. If you're leaving you'd better do it soon."

"But I have to go with you. You told Mother—"

I stared at her, realizing suddenly that it wouldn't be as easy as I thought it would—and with Beth along— God, what was I getting her into? But she didn't look like she'd budge. Well, hell! "Suit yourself." It would be a long trip back to Illana.

"Thank you, I will."

Later, after putting the suit away, I paused to listen to the corgen. In flight the Gabby's core purred soft as a contented kitten, but in the atmosphere of Minder the corgen shook the Gabby's frame hard enough to make me worry for her safety. Even on Minder's fantastic gravity grid at one-third Gs the Gabby labored like an asthmatic old lady, but at least the rough edges seemed to be smoothing out.

Then, thinking of the small hole someone had punched into the Gabby's outer layers, my anger deepened, and the throbbing in my cheek increased. If a man wants to be miserable he can find a lot of excuses.

In the lounge again Beth took a look at me. "You're angry."

"You damned well better believe it." The compboard on the control panel chimed and—God!—how I hoped it was our clearance to leave.

It was. "This is Term-Con," said Terminal Control. "You now have lift-off clearance." He went on to give me a rundown of traffic in the area. I recorded it for future use. "You will hear a tone," he concluded, "at which time the grid reached maximum minus and you can use your maneuvering pods to clear the field. Please don't go to full power within twenty-two thousand KKs."

"Right-o, Term-Con." I thought he was through. He wasn't.

"Oh, by the way. We also have an LT transmission for you from Illana. Can you run it through?"

"One minute, Control." From Illana it could be Pete, or maybe Dunn. I stored the traffic data and flipped on the scrambler and once more punched the record button. "Okay, run her through."

Term-con transmitted a quick series of high-pitched sqawks and squeals that lasted approximately five seconds. Then, "Do you need a repeat?"

"I'll take repeat for good measure." Always a good idea to get a backup when possible. Term-con repeated the five second bleep and when it finished the face in the view-com actually smiled. "Good bye, Captain Corbett. We look forward to your next visit."

Probably told that to all the departing ships.

With the help of Minder's tremendous grid the Gabby lifted from the planet's surface slowly, majestically, and the further we rose, the easier I breathed. I'd been haunted by the fear that the Marquessa wouldn't let us go, but if Beth held a similar thought, it didn't show.

At twenty-two thousand KKs I kicked the retros in and pulled her around into a moon orbit. Above our heads the Minder sun was a big red ball, and to our left at a steady distance were the tandem moons. Below was the dusty, glowing surface of the desert planet. Hard to remember the beauty of the Bells at this distance.

"Why are we stopping?" Beth followed me down the passageway to storage.

"I have a repair job, remember?" I pulled on the black and white striped space suit and air pack. Hauled down the con-light and tool box.

"But don't you want to read the LT from Illana? It might be something important."

I frowned. I hadn't forgotten. I just wanted to save it until the work was done. But she was like a kid with an unopened present. I shrugged. "Run it through the transcriber if you want. I won't be out too long."

Patching the hull of a ship isn't hard, but it's tedious. Each layer, piece by piece, had to be built up and welded. It's strictly dumb work, using the con-light and repair unit and muscles in your body you usually don't know are there. It's work that leaves the mind free to play. To wander. I kept thinking of Pete who was enjoying life on Illana while I travelled halfway across the Cluster. But that wasn't fair, either, and I knew it. I was where I wanted to be. Out here, with the universe around me, a starview that no planet in the universe could give. There wasn't any way I could do what Pete did, day after day cooped up in an office with figures and machines and computers that said whether or not you were making money. Hell, with a job like Pete's I'd go crazy. I had to be out here. I *had* to be. Even when the jobs were dull, repetitious, tedious and frustrating.

My patch job took the full hours I'd allotted to it, and by the time I was through, a small measure of peace had returned to me. Dunn was wrong. Maybe our small branch of the human race would never be reunited with the rest of humanity. Maybe this surrounding Cluster was all we'd ever have. Maybe there was no miracle fuel or different kind of propulsion system that'd take us back the way our ancestors had come.

But if Dunn was wrong to think our progress meant just more speed, what about those people who worshipped the past with a religious intensity that sometimes approached fanaticism? Those who'd made the Nathan Gorham Museum a shrine? At least Dunn's look was more the future than that,

And where was I in it all? Right in the middle! That happy middle where we could exist in the here-and-now and enjoy it!

And if it was that desire to enjoy life that had made Ken call me a stardrifter, then stardrifter I was, and stardrifter I'd always be.

Feeling better, I hauled the tools in.

Beth met me in the passageway before I even had all the tools through the connector. "Gil, the message—"

"Who was it from? Pete, I'll bet. How's he doing?"

"He—he—" She couldn't finish. She handed me the printout.

I'd been wrong. It was from Gordy Pittman

Pete attacked in office two nights ago. Intruders took some paperwork. Will keep you informed of any change in his condition.

My sense of peace fled. I stared at the paper. He'd keep us informed? It had an ominous sound.

"Gil—"

The words on the printout blurred. I couldn't look at Beth. Why hadn't I told Pete to be careful? What could anyone take from the office that would be that important?

"I'm sorry, Gil. Is there anything we can do?"

"No." Nothing. Not from here. Gordy and Dunn would have to look after him.

So senseless! Nothing important . . .

I kicked the tightsuit off and threw it in the cupboard, then pushed past Beth to the lounge. Time to get on with the job. Accept the attack on Pete for what it was. A warning that from now on things could get rough.

"Don't worry, Gil. He'll be all right. I know he will."

Sure he would. But what about us?

7

Entering the Brothers System five days later, I still wasn't sure what would happen to us, but at least my anger had faded and I could talk to Beth without biting at her. We hadn't had any more transmissions, and as my great-grandmother Dorrie always used to say, no news is good—sometimes.

The hour badge said Afternoon Six, Star Time, when we reached the outer boundaries and started our inward spiral toward Brother Timothy. A day out of Minder's Portals we'd passed a group of patrol ships, Minder-based, and had exchanged identification, but since then we hadn't passed another ship. At A-4 we'd crossed over the Brother's defense screen, and identified for them, so they knew we were on our way in. But actual contact didn't come until we approached the parking spheres, a day after we first entered the system, and then it was just an official order to use Ball-10, the sphere above Timothy's one and only city.

I acknowledged the order and we docked, and then I opened the nose shields so we could see the surface. But before we had time to do more than pick up the lights thousands of KKs below, the view com spoke again. A female voice. This time I put her on the screen.

A dark haired, narrow faced woman appeared. She was familiar in a mind-teasing way, but before I had time to puzzle it out she identified herself. "Good evening, Captain Corbett. You've made good time on your trip from Illana. I am Allia Balik."

Balik? Of course. Strong family resemblance, especially around the cold eyes. "Good evening, Min Balik. I trust your brother is doing well in Illana?"

"Yes, thank you. *I* trust your trip was a pleasant one."

I thought of the two ships that had awaited us outside the Minder Portals, and lied. "Quite."

After a short pause Min Balik's mouth smiled, sending a little chill down my back. "You'll please stand by for three Treasury Department Officials who will come aboard to inspect your cargo."

Damn it, I thought, here we go again! "Madam, I have no cargo. As I explained to your brother in Illana, I've not come to trade. I carry nothing but the shipment for which your brother contracted. Other than to make sure it's all there, I can't see that it needs inspecting."

"I'm sorry. No ship can come in without being inspected and paying for same."

"It's not in the contract, Madam—"

"It doesn't need to be. It's law."

"And what's your fee for that?"

"Five thousand credits. There's also a matter of parking fee."

"Yes, one thousand a day. I already know."

"Payable daily—"

From the other side of the lounge Beth grinned, but I ignored her. If the Brothers wanted to be this way, I could put up with it. Especially if we could unload the damned gold and get out of here!

Min Balik had hesitated, now she went on. 'We will

82

also take possession of the shipment as soon as possible."

"Fine." I started to relax. "How soon will that be?"

"In a day or two. We do not at the moment have a shuttle available for that weight."

If that wasn't a bunch of bull!

"In the meantime," she continued, "you and your *wife* are welcome to spend a few days in the city as guests of our High Committee."

And how much would they charge us for that? But it was only a passing thought. Anyone who thought I'd leave the ship was out of his/her head. "I'm sorry to refuse your hospitality, Min Balik, but as long as the shipment's on board I'll have to stay with it. When will your inspection team be here?"

Her eyes grew colder. "One is already on the way. You will stand by to receive them." The screen went blank.

Beth made a face. "Aggressive, isn't she?"

"You recognize the type?"

Beth swung facing me, her eyes suddenly fiery. "I'm not like that, Gil Corbett, and I resent the implication."

"Tough." I turned back to First Control.

Behind me Beth stomped down the length of the lounge and the door to the sleeper slid loudly shut.

Not quite an hour after Min Balik appeared on our viewscreen the star-comp warned of an approaching ship. I'd punched in for soup and sandwiches and called Beth to supper when the bell went off and startled me so badly I almost spilled soup in my lap. It was much too soon for the shuttle bringing the inspection team, and I put a star view on the screen to see what has happening.

The bell brought Beth out of her sleeper. "What is

it?"

I pointed at the screen. "Ship coming in." A big Class Six! Federation! What in the hell were they doing here? I changed the power on the screen and we could read the name on her side. The Eagle. Three times as big as the Gabby, and twice as hard to maneuver, but her pilot was good. I had to admit. He made parking her look easy. It took no longer to bring her nose in than it'd taken me with the Gabby.

Watching, I thought, why not? They've always got the best. Best ships, best pilots. Great life, if you liked playing soldiers. But not me. I'd tried it years before. Tried it, then gotten out as fast as I could.

Then, remembering the shadow ship that'd followed us from Illana, I was no longer hungry. Could it be this one? But what reason—instantly the Marquessa came to mind. Did she—? Did the Marquessa of Sandyminder swing that much weight? Had she finagled Federation protection for her precious daughter? I laughed out loud.

Beth's mouth tightened. "What's so funny?"

"Do you know there's only twenty-five Federation vessels in the whole Cluster? I think it's funnier than hell one just happens to be here now. I didn't know your mother swung that much weight."

Beth flushed. "She doesn't."

"Then it's one hell of a coincidence, love, and I don't believe in coincidence."

The com-board chimed. A new caution made me put it on the big screen. I wanted to see who called before I answered.

A man in Federation blue and white appeared and an electric sense of danger shot through me.

Mike Pelonyi? My apprehension returned full force. According to Dunn, it was Mike who'd been checking on the Gabby! I punched the com and identified.

"Federation First Officer Pelonyi," he replied, "requesting permission to come aboard the Trading Vessel Gabriella."

"Officially?" I don't know why I asked. Nothing could sound more official than his tone.

"Officially," he confirmed.

Damn it, why hadn't I questioned Dunn more closely about that visit? I'd known Mike a long time. Friends I knew we weren't. Not since Ken's disappearance. And now he looked as friendly as—as I felt! Thinking of my possible choices I shook my head. "Permission denied." I damned well wouldn't let Federation board me!

Beth's spoon clattered against her bowl, and Mike blinked his surprise. A small muscle in his jaw twitched. "On what grounds do you deny permission, Trader?"

"On the grounds that I've not been charged with any Federation offense, and I'm not a member of the Trader's convention, and until I am one or the other it's my prerogative to invite or dis-invite whomsoever I choose aboard my ship."

Looking remote, Mike nodded. "Very well. I'll pass the word along."

"You do that."

I reached out and switched the big screen to starview. Already a crew surrounded the Eagle's tail, cleaning jets or something. But that was standard operating procedure with a ship as big as this Federation bird.

Beth pushed her bowl away. "Gil, what do you mean talking to a Federation officer like that? He could arrest you."

"I doubt it." I stared up at the screen. Why were they here? Were they staying awhile? Why did he want to come aboard "officially?"

Ten minutes passed. Beth started to pace. Then the com-board chimed again.

"Request permission," Mike said with a serious face, "to come aboard the Gabby in an unofficial capacity as friend of the Captain."

Friend of the—he had to be kidding. But he didn't look like it. Watching him, I tried to still my increasing uneasiness, but with no success. Should I let him aboard? Well, why not? Maybe I'd get some answers out of him. Like, why was he on Quintus checking on the Gabby? Or what was he doing here?

I nodded abruptly. "Come aboard."

In the passageway beside the connector half an hour later I introduced Beth to Mike. "Beth, this is Mike Pelonyi, of the Federation." Mike shot me a quizzical look. "Mike," I continued very politely, "this is my wife, Beth."

Mike had started to bend over Beth's hand in the grand service manner, but he jerked up straight, his eyes wide. "Wife? You, Gil?" But it sounded false. I knew him too well.

I gave him a mean smile. "Even die-hard traders get lonesome, Mike."

"Especially die-hard traders, I should guess." Mike still held Beth's hand. He smiled at her.

Mike is big, handsome, and makes quite an impression on the girls. At least this time Beth acted impressed. She smiled and withdrew from his grasp. "Welcome aboard the Gabby, Officer Pelonyi."

"Please." He mock frowned. "Please call me Mike. You seem familiar. Have we met before?"

A coolness entered Beth's voice. "No, I'm sure I'd remember if we'd ever met."

They both irritated me. "If you're through trying to impress my wife, Mike, I'll offer you an unofficial drink."

Shooting me an unreadable look, Beth turned and preceded us down the passageway to the lounge.

Mike took a place at the table in the lounge and I pulled a drink from the dispenser in the galley. When I set it in front of him, I asked the question straight out. "Why did you want to come aboard officially?"

"My commander wants to know what the hell you're doing here." He tossed the drink down and smiled at Beth. "Just curious."

Nosey was more like it. "That's the service mentality. Never ask if you can demand, right?"

Beth ignored me. "Who is your commander?"

Mike studied his glass, turned it this way and that as thought judging the quality. "Joshua Sinclair." He glanced at me and away again. "Best damned Commander in the Service."

"That's not saying much for the service is it?" I asked. Sinclair was the one who'd testified at the insurance hearing to keep us from collecting on the 'Bella's loss. I laughed to hide my rising temper. "You're a long way from home, aren't you? How long've you been out this time?"

"Six months. Hey, Gil," Mike's eyes turned suddenly sympathetic. "Did you ever hear about your brother and his ship? That sure was a tough break."

Sure it was. And tougher because the damned Federation—"No, never did." Six months did he say? The damned liar! "At least nothing we could pin down."

At that moment a jar ran through the Gabby's hull and a cargo door alarm went off. I was halfway out of my chair when Mike said, "Sit down, Gil. You're being boarded."

Staring at him, I sank back into the chair. Choking. "Damn you, Mike! I'll take this to the highest Court on Illana. The Federation has no right—"

"We do if we suspect smuggling."

"Smuggling?" A movement from Beth made me glance at her. A hand covered her hour badge. She was white and angry. But she saw me looking and turned away.

I faced Mike again. "Smuggling what, for God's sake? I've got a legitimate shipment on board and the papers to prove it."

"In that case we'll apologize."

"You'll do it in court, by God."

"Gil, who paid you five hundred thousand credits gold?"

"Why don't you ask who paid me six million, six hundred thousand, Mike?"

His eyes narrowed. "Okay. Who?"

"Go to hell!" I looked at Beth again. She'd recovered from the first shock and now was red in the face. The haughty autocrat in her was showing. I thought she'd say something to Mike in that marquessa tone of hers, but instead she rose, walked past us both and disappeared into the big sleeper.

Mike followed her progress, his look mildly appreciative. "You've got good taste, Gil, but then you always did."

Oh hell! How could he talk like that when the whole world was falling apart? I leaned my face into my hands and tried to think. Something important—something important I should be thinking of—something that wouldn't come to mind but that gave me a cold prickle of fear!

What in the hell was going on? This was the second time in seven days I'd been accused of smuggling. On Sandy they'd thought I was smuggling gold. What did the Federation think I had on board? "Mike, what are you looking for?"

"Don't you know?" His voice was suddenly hard.

"Would I be asking if I did?"

"Dithalium chloride."

I stared at him. DTC? Me? I wanted to laugh, but I couldn't. He was serious. "Me, Mike? You think I'd—" Then the horror of it hit me. Mike could honestly believe I'd smuggle something as deadly as DTC?

He did. His eyes were accusatory. It hurt, the thought that he could even suspect me. I shrugged. "Okay, you think I have DTC aboard, you have my permission to take this ship apart bolt by bolt, seam by seam. For all the good it'll do you." Not that he looked like he was awaiting my permission. "And then," I went on, "by God, you'll get off my ship!" I tried to sound calm, but I didn't have much success. My mind raced. Why had I even let him on board? How stupid could I be? Or would they have boarded anyway? I glanced at Mike's hard face. Probably so.

But I also felt something else, though it was no consolation. Mike didn't look like he enjoyed what he was doing.

What seemed a long time later, but might've been only minutes, a uniformed service type came down the passageway from cargo. Grimly he saluted Mike and handed him a slate.

Mike stared at it, then at the service man. "Are you sure?"

"Yes, sir."

"Then open up the drums."

They'd found the fuel in Cargo Three. I almost said be careful, but thought better of it. That was his responsibility. Let him worry whether or not any of his men would get a rad overdose.

Mike turned to me. "You said you had a legitimate cargo on board. Where?"

I sat silent in my chair. Should I or shouldn't I show

him?

If I didn't I might very well end up in the Eagle's brig. Slowly I stood. "I'll show you." Calling his men, Mike followed me down the passage.

The gravity floor grids on a normal Class Four aren't removable. The floor grids on the Gabby's Cargo One area are.

Once we entered Cargo One it took only a quick touch in the proper sequence on the seven-button control hidden in the panelling to unlock the middle module of the floor grid, and I lifted the light, closely woven grid without effort. The flat, rectangular chests, six of them side by side, were stuck tight to the grid and weightless in the disturbed gravity field. I pointed to them and the contempt I felt was in my voice. "Go ahead, Mike. Open them."

If he was surprised with the smuggler's cove, he covered well. He nodded at his two men and they moved in on the boxes.

I experienced only a momentary fear, but it passed with the opening of the first chest. Gold! The sparkling, beautiful newly minted gold coin of the Brothers.

Mike dropped to one knee and picked out a floating coin. Then frowned at me. "Do you have trading papers on this?"

"I told you. I'm delivering. On contract. If you'll check with your Federation agent on Illana he'll find the original contract in Illana Central's vault."

Feeling the muscles tighten across my shoulders, I tried to smile. "There's also another 6.1 mil waiting for me to produce the delivery receipt. Which'll be mine when the Brothers Treasury Agents come for their gold."

"No," said Beth in a brittle voice from the passage door. "No it won't!"

8

Beth?

I turned.

Standing in the doorway from Storage, Beth held the deadliest small hand weapon made. A short barrel LEM. Light-emitting matrix. And she held it so I had no doubt she knew how to use it.

I didn't ask what she was doing. That would've been superfluous.

I stilled a brush of panic, and I drew a deep breath.

The LEM encompassed the four of us: me, Mike and the two Federation Servicemen. But Beth watched only me. "Well, why don't you say something?"

My racing mind slid by whole blocks of unspoken questions. "I don't talk to ladies holding LEMs." Immediately the old saw "That's no lady, that's my wife" came to mind. The thought should've been funny, but it hurt.

Beth shifted the LEM as though it were growing heavy. "Too bad. We have a little while to wait."

"For what?" Mike asked. But he, too, was careful not to move.

"For some friends who'll remove this gold. You've no idea, Gil, how hard I've searched, trying to find where you hid it."

"Why didn't you ask?"

"You wouldn't have told me."

"Oh," I forced a smile, "I would have. I'm pretty godawful dumb about some things." Like falling in love, to mention one. And if this wasn't the master con of Nathan Gorham's tenth century, I didn't know what was!

Slowly Mike came to his feet. "After you've taken the gold, what'll you do?"

Beth's eyes grew darker. "Whatever has to be done."

Mike's two men were still half-bent over the boxes, ludicrous expressions on their faces. With the LEM, Beth motioned them toward the door to Cargo Two and they moved. Fast. I didn't blame them. I glanced at Mike, and he too had apparently assessed Beth's ability to use the weapon. When she told him to lock the door after his men, he did so with no argument.

Which left the floor grid free of interference.

Now was the only chance I'd have, and I knew it. Not a chance at Beth and the LEM, but at getting the gold once more under lock and key. And not much of a chance at that. Watching Beth's eyes flick from Mike back to me, I took my chance anyway.

I threw myself sideways and down across the grid. Covering my face, I fell flat on the raised flooring, pushing it downward until the floor locks clicked into place.

A brilliant flash filled the Cargo room. The same moment the lock clicked, a fiery pain shot down my left leg, tearing at my nerves, pulling a painful yell from my soul.

When I could lift my head again, neither Beth nor Mike had moved, and both were watching me. Mike's hand was still on the lock to Cargo Two.

"Get up!" Beth's voice was shaky.

Carefully I did as she said. I'd never had a LEM

wound before, but I'd heard enough about them to be glad I was still alive. She could've torn my whole leg off. I didn't even look down. "Go ahead and kill me, Beth. Then you'll never have the gold."

"I'm not a murderer, Gil. Not unless you make me one." She studied the closed floor grid. "I suppose you had a good reason for that?"

Mike laughed. It was a small, tense sound. I forced a smile. "Yes, Love, I really did."

She glanced down at her hour badge and frowned. Gesturing with the LEM she pointed us at the passageway. "Go into the lounge. We'll wait there."

"For inspection team?" I guessed. She nodded. That figured, didn't it? And what of Balik? Was he in on it too?

While I wondered, Mike moved by me toward the passageway through storage. He, at least, seemed to have acknowledged that whatever Beth wanted, Beth got.

When we reached the lounge I fell into the nearest recliner. It was getting harder to pretend I didn't hurt. Nerve endings developed where there had been none before, but I clamped my jaw. I'd not give Beth the satisfaction of knowing how much damage she'd done. Not to my leg and not to me!

Mike stopped at my side. "You all right? Can I help you?"

"Get lost, Pelonyi." If he hadn't believed I'd carry DTC this wouldn't have happened!

Mike turned to Beth. "He needs help for that hole you put in his leg, lady. Where's the doc-box?"

All ships carry a doctor's box, but I knew Beth didn't have any idea where ours was. I was right. Beth's face became more drawn, but she shook her head. "I haven't the slightest idea." She motioned with the LEM to the other recliner. "Sit down, Mr.

93

Pelonyi. It won't be much longer."

Mike pointed at the large viewscreen. "Damn it, don't you realize a Federation ship's out there, and it's waiting to hear from me?"

Beth smiled slightly. "Are you that important?"

The next forty-five minutes passed in agonizing slowness. For once Mike seemed to find nothing to say and that didn't hurt my feelings. The pain in my leg made me nauseous and the lights of the lounge grew too bright. It hurt me almost as much that I couldn't figure out Beth's motive for all this. Was she in league with the Brothers? Well, some of them, anyway.

Drifting numbly, my mind was at some distant place when an idea shot into my head so audacious it made that passage between the two pirate ships outside Minder's Portals look like child's play. It brought me sharply back to reality. Could I get away with it? Did they want the gold that badly? I wouldn't have the delivery receipt for the rest of our fee from Illana Central, but did that matter? If I could trade the gold—for Ken and the Bella—

For the first time since he disappeared, thinking about Ken brought no painful tightness to my throat. *Here was something I could do!*

The chiming compboard broke into my thoughts. Beth flipped the panel into open and again Min Balik's narrow face appeared on the screen.

Balik looked worried. Beth smiled tightly. "Come aboard, Allia. Everything's under control."

"But there's a Federation shuttle docked on the first Cargo Port."

"It's been taken care of."

Balik nodded and the screen went back to the starview.

Nervously rubbing the back of his neck, Mike

spoke into the silence. "Just what do you expect to do, Mrs. Corbett? It's impossible for your people to take that gold. Absolutely—"

I cut him off with a frown. "You're wasting your breath."

Beth shook her head. Now that Balik's arrival was imminent, she seemed to feel better. "You surprise me, Gil. I thought you'd be furious."

Furious? Too mild a word for what I felt! But it would get me nowhere to let her know it.

I smiled. "You want me to rant and rave? I'm not the type."

I moved slightly and pain knifed up my leg. I shut my eyes and took a deep breath.

"No," said Beth, "you're not the type." She sounded angry.

Mike stood. "Gil, where's that damned box?"

God, I couldn't go any longer without some kind of help! "In the cupboard under that tape shelf."

Ignoring the fact that Beth's fingers turned white around the LEM, Mike pulled out the box and knelt by my side.

The wound wasn't large, about the size of Mike's Service belt buckle, but it had a strong, sweetish smell. Mike sprayed it with deadening mist then placed a dressing over it. "Any plastiskin?"

"No." Never had any need for it.

"Any goddamn painkillers?"

"Some daylon, I think." Mike found the box of capsules and I swallowed a couple cold. Dropped the rest into my pocket.

Grimly Mike finished up and shoved the chest back into its cupboard. I didn't thank him.

Min Balik and a young man came aboard just after Mike finished. The Balik woman was older than Beth,

95

and where Beth had been merely proficient with the LEM, Balik seemed to enjoy the feel of it.

"Gil Corbett and Federation Officer Mike Pelonyi," Beth said. "Min Allia Balik and Ed White."

White? I gave him a quick glance. Handsome kid. Brawny. But somehow not the type I thought Beth would go for. Whatever that type was.

Nodding at the introduction, Mike leaned back on the edge of the star-comp table, his arms crossed in front of him as though this being boarded were a simple, everyday occurrence. Having suffered it twice in one day, somehow I couldn't be so nonchalant.

Not pausing for conversation, Beth led the Balik woman aft. "It's back here." They left White to watch us.

I blinked through my haze at Beth's intended. "Edward White? Edward Randall White? *The* Edward—"

He stared at me and so did the LEM in his hand. "What of it?"

This was the guy Beth said she was supposed to marry? It looked to me as though she deserved him! How dumb could I be? Why hadn't I questioned her story? How could I be so stupid? I shook my head and glanced down at my leg. At least I'd never wonder again how she really felt. The painful evidence was easy to read.

I tried to relax, but my mind raced. I thought of my earlier idea. Of course! They'd changed the players, so I could change the rules. But would they deal with me? How badly did they want that gold? Bad enough to trade it for Ken and the Arabella?

Mike straightened. He seemed to have made a decision. "This is the damnedest thing I've ever heard of. Aren't you taking a great chance, White, with that Federation ship less than a kilometer away?"

White laughed at him. "The Federation doesn't scare us, Mon Pelonyi. Not any more than does the Trader here."

"I've never tried to scare anyone," I said.

"You would deliver this gold to the Committee coffers with no pang of conscience—"

"I've delivered it, not made a moral judgment on it."

"Yes, you've delivered it." He smiled. "To us."

"Not quite." Where in the hell was the real Brothers delegation. Why hadn't that Federation ship become curious?

A slight movement from Mike caught my attention. A tensing. His hands had dropped to his belt. Damn it, he was starting to move on White! He'd ruin everything! "Hey Pelonyi," I said, "sit down and relax. They aren't going anywhere for a while."

As I intended, my words drew White's attention to Mike, and the LEM which had stared at me so steadily turned its large eye in his direction. White's face tightened. "Sit down Officer Pelonyi. You make me nervous."

Shooting me a black look, Mike sat.

A short moment later Beth reappeared in the galley arch, cat mad, "All right, Gil, how does it open?"

I grinned at her. "I told you, Beth, you only had to ask."

Frowning, she brough her anger under control. "Come show me then."

"No, not now."

Min Balik appeared beyond Beth's shoulder, her eyes as lethal as the LEM in her hand. "You don't have a choice. You'll tell us or we'll kill you."

"Then," I pointed out, "you'll never get it." Which probably wasn't true, but were they smart enough to know that?

Beth raised the LEM and turned it on Mike, her pale face sternly set. "Then we'll kill your friend."

Was she bluffing? I didn't care. "Go ahead. He's no friend of mine." With satisfaction, I saw Mike tense. "You might remember, though," I continued before she could take me seriously, "that killing me would only be a system offense. Killing an officer of the Federation might get you into trouble."

Impatiently Beth waved the LEM. "What does that mean?"

White grabbed her hand and forced it down. "Corbett's right, Beth. We'd have every ship in the Federation landing on us."

"But—" I grinned again. "I'm willing to bargain."

Mike jerked around to stare at me, protest on his face. A brittle silence filled the lounge. Then Min Balik whispered, "What is it you want?"

I thought they'd never ask. "I'll trade that gold in Cargo One for my brother Ken Corbett and his ship, the Arabella."

Beth's mouth tightened. "But he's probably dead. You said so yourself!"

"If he's dead, then I want his body."

Min Balik's cold look met mine. A chill touched me. Had I misjudged them? Her words came in small, savage bites. "And—the—ship?"

"My brother's ship. The Arabella."

"You want them in return for this gold?" She flushed angrily. "You're delirious. Where would we—"

"That's your problem. You deliver and I'll gladly give you every last gold coin!" And it'd be worth all the money in trust at Illana Central to have them returned. Of course it would. We weren't meant to be rich anyway.

Beth's eyes flashed fire. "You meant to do this all

the time!"

I grinned at her. Let her think so. I didn't care.

Min Balik stared at me. "But how can you do that? The gold isn't yours to bargain with."

"It isn't yours, either, Min Balik."

Min Balik's mouth became a thin, tight line. She motioned Beth and White toward the Galley out of earshot and they conferred.

After a long moment of thoughtful silence, Mike leaned forward, whispering, "Do you know what the hell you've started, Gil?"

I ignored him.

Mike tried again. "Gil, you don't know what they have in mind. We can't just sit here. Don't you have a weapon of some kind? We could take them—"

And Mike was just stupid enough to try. "Save your breath, Pelonyi. Federation has done enough damage without your messing this up, too."

Mike flushed. "Do you know what you're doing?"

"Damned right. What the Federation should've done six months ago." Rather than argue, I changed the subject. "Mike, who told you that lie about my smuggling DTC?"

"We got the rumor in Illana." He had the grace to look embarrassed. "Our informant said it was being shipped in crystal form and hidden in a wood sculpture. If we were wrong—"

I didn't hear the rest. DTC hidden in a wooden sculpture? Beth's? Setting me up, goddammit, that was a charge a man'd never live down!

I thought again of those few minutes in the hovercar on the way back from the Marquessa's Hall. Beth had known even then . . . But why would she—how could she—?

"Gil, are you all right?"

I blinked and Mike's tense face came into focus.

"Yeah, I'm all right." More all right than I'd been for some time, maybe. And I still had a couple of ships and Ken to worry about.

Down from the Galley passageway Beth's voice rose sharply. "We can make that decision ourselves."

"No!" Min Balik also forgot to whisper. "We'll take it up with Garrison." Abruptly the voices dropped. Looking at the angry trio gathered by the Galley arch, I shivered. Who was Garrison? Would he be the one to find Ken and the 'Bella? How soon would we know?

The answers were slow in coming. Three hours later, after a stomach-dropping descent to the planet surface, we were lost some place in that vast array of lights we'd seen from above. The air was heavy and cold, but in spite of the bright lights there were no people on the streets.

Min Balik, winning the argument with Beth, had ordered Mike to contact his ship and inform his captain he was accompanying us to the surface, and Mike had obeyed without hesitation. I got the impression he thought he was going along to keep me out of trouble. How Beth and her friends expected to remain undetected beat me. The two crewmen were still locked in Cargo Two, and surely someone would come looking for them before too long. But maybe, just maybe, Beth's group didn't care. This was a system matter, and a system which was not a member of the FIS at that. Federation had no jurisdiction as long as their men weren't hurt.

Finally we were hustled into a dark doorway, down some stairs and into a dark hall filled with people. My eyes took time to become accustomed to the dimness, but once I could see I realized we'd been brought into a kind of theater. A cabaret. White took my arm and pushed me through a maze of cubicles toward a back hallway.

An acrid smell permeated the air, and at the other end of the cabaret a woman caught in a bright light did a slow strip to unheard music. Each person in the audience, sitting in his isolated little booth, watched without a sideward glance at our passage.

Depressing. Sick.

A few steps later we reached a room that was a shade lighter than the gloom we'd just come through. White released my arm and brushed his hands as though he'd been contaminated by touching me. "You'll wait here."

"Sure, if you say so." What choice did I have?

Mike appeared then in the doorway, stumbling as though he'd been pushed. White repeated his warning and Mike's nod was a blur in the grey light. White disappeared and the doorway took on a faint, bluish glow like the soft glow of the core at minimum level.

"I'll be damned," Mike said. "A Delta field." He turned to me. "You know, those things are so new the Federation is just now modifying the ships for them."

I grunted but didn't ask what a Delta field was. With Mike that'd be like opening the faucet and then breaking the handle. And I wasn't that interested. I had other problems to worry about. Why had Beth tried to get Federation to pick me up on a DTC charge? To get me out of the way so they could take the gold? Or was I supposed to be arrested by some Brothers official? Yes, that seemed more likely. Leave it to the Federation to foul up everyone's plans! But— the thought left me cold—that would mean Beth was working for— but that didn't make any sense. She wouldn't—but obviously she was!

Mike moved closer. "How's your leg?"

"Sore." The walking since we'd come to surface

hadn't helped a bit.

"You know," Mike dropped his voice to a whisper, "I'd swear I smelled DTC when we came through that joint."

"You've got DTC on the brain!" I knew what he was doing. He wanted a reason to bring the Federation down on this group. But it wouldn't work. The most Federation could do would be to inform the Brothers officialdom what they'd found. Their authority wasn't worth a hollow credit here, and even Mike knew it!

Mike moved away, pacing the perimeter of the small room like a restless cat. "Gil, what makes you think they'll give you the 'Bella in return for the gold?"

"I think the gold's worth it to them."

"That's stupid. They'll not give you anything if they can help it!"

"You're pretty damned stupid yourself, if you'd believe I'd carry DTC." Every time I thought about that, it made me mad all over again.

Mike ignore me. "Lucky as hell for you that we're sitting where we are up there!"

That gave me pause, because he was right. I might be dead right now, instead of merely wounded, if Mike hadn't come aboard when he did. But that still didn't make me like it any better.

Mike stopped in front of me again. "What makes you think they haven't dismantled and junked the 'Bella already?"

"She's too valuable."

"Crap. If they kept her they wouldn't have anyone who could run with her modifications."

I stared at him through the gloom, a cold stillness settling on me. What did he know about the 'Bella's modifications?

"Besides—" he went on.

I had to shut him up. What if someone was listening? I doubled up and fell forward. "Mike! Help me!"

He caught me before I hit the floor. "What's the matter? Your leg?"

"Just need—in my pocket—the daylon—"

A long low chest sat along one wall. Mike helped me to it. "You need a doctor, dammit." He gave me one of capsules and I swallowed it gratefully. I really had needed it, Mike slammed his hand against the wall. "You can come back to the Eagle with me. We've got the best damned doctor in the fleet."

"No thanks, Pelonyi. I need Federation's help like I need another hole in my leg." I shut my eyes and leaned against the cold wall. Damn him anyway. What did he know about those modifications?

"Gil," Mike's tone was conciliatory, "can I ask a question?"

"Could I stop you?" If he mentioned the Bella again I'd hit him.

Tightly he laughed. "I guess not!" He sounded embarrassed. "Ah, are you really married?"

His question caught me off guard. The ache I felt had nothing to do with legs or LEMs, and it wasn't anything the little pain capsules could help. "Yes," I said. "Yes, I am."

White returned, saving us from any further effort at conversation.

9

Unfamiliar with the terrain of Brother Timothy, I couldn't begin to say where we were headed, but we left the City in the direction opposite the shuttle field where we'd landed. Not blessed with a good ground sense when I can't see the sky, I was soon lost by the twisting and turning of our black-windowed hovercar.

Numbly I leaned back in a corner and tried to keep myself awake by remembering all the things I'd heard about this system.

The first monks who'd come seeking solitude in this outer corner of the Cluster had found a two-star five planet system, of which one planet was habitable. The first stardrifters, those space gypsies who had been chased out here also sought solitude, on their own when the inner circle of stars in the Cluster became too regulated for their liking.

Habitable, perhaps, but not pleasant or productive.

It was at best a base for pirates preying on other systems. It couldn't support itself any other way.

Jerking to a stop, the hovercar's interior lights blinked on. The driver, a middle-aged man with grey, curling hair, turned and gave us a hard look. Min Balik, sitting directly behind him, whispered in his ear. He nodded and pointed to a compartment by the door. Staring at him, a stillness grew in me.

Hovercar and driver?

Delta field?

What kind of an organization was this?

White fit a blindfold over my eyes, and in the ensuing darkness I considered further questions. Who were they? What did they really want? Was it only the gold?

The hovercar stopped again some time later, and Beth and her friends marched us, still blindfolded, up a steeply graded pathway that felt rough to my feet. Dirt, maybe, or fine gravel. When we reached the top it changed to smooth pavement, and then we started down again.

This time steps, and Beth's hand on my arm to guide me. I chilled to her touch and anger almost blotted out my pain.

Finally Min Balik drew a halt. "Far enough. Remove the blindfolds."

I squinted in bright light. We stood at the back of a large, empty lecture hall. Almost empty. A group of people below us clustered around a man on the podium. From our position he seemed old and bent.

Silvernight? All other thoughts vanished from my mind. Silvernight! It had to be! That hair—it had to be! Of course!

My certainty grew. Below us the group split up, some going down a stairway behind the stage, others proceeding out along one aisle. The old man was left alone. Glancing up as though he was just now aware of our presence, he gathered a sheaf of papers from a lectern, ducked his head and scurried away.

Beth gasped. "Why that's the man you were speaking of, Gil. Silver—Silvernight?"

I nodded.

"Oh no!" Sharply Min Balik laughed. "That's Lorsa Connat. He teaches here. You remember, Beth, I told you about him."

Beth laughed too. Relief cleared her eyes. "Of course. Lorsa Connat."

Min Balik stared at the departing figure, her face once more that cold, still mask. Who was she trying to kid? It *was* Silvernight. I'd bet my last credit on that! Mike, catching my glance, crooked a quizzical brow. He knew, too.

Min Balik led us down the broad aisle toward that empty stage, and our steps echoed against the rising tiers of seats.

I studied the stage where Silvernight had so recently stood. An enlarger screen stood across the back, and the lectern carried a projector. I'd seen them on Illana. So accoustically well designed that a word whispered in front of it would be heard clearly to the very back row. And every expression, every nuance, would be plain as day.

I put Silvernight on that screen, examined his face. Remembered him as I'd seen him on Illana addressing a group of industrial synthesizers. An expert among experts. Diffident, brilliant and a little sad. Damn it, the man we'd just seen *was* Silvernight! No matter what they called him here.

"Gil!" Impatiently Beth pushed at me. "This way, please."

Slowly I followed Mike down through the door below the podium. This was the way Silvernight had gone. Would we see him again? I hoped so. He was a link to the 'Bella, if not to Ken himself!

We travelled only a short way down before White stopped at a door with a small visiplate, and announced our arrival. The door opened and he ushered us through.

Inside the room the five of us were a crowd. Min Balik and White looked at each other, and Min Balik shrugged. "I'll do it." Whatever it was, she looked reluctant.

White's smile hardened. He turned to Mike. "Mr. Pelonyi, you will come with me."

Mike's jaw set. "Nothing doing. I'm sticking right here with Corbett."

"That's not possible." White eyed me coldly. "Please tell him—"

I glanced at Mike. He was getting tiresome. "How many times do I have to tell you, this guy is no friend!"

Mike's smile didn't conceal the steel in his eyes. "How many times do I have to remind all of you that Trader Corbett is under suspicion of smuggling DTC, which is a Federation offense. Until I prove otherwise—"

I turned my back on him, and the mere act of turning sent an agonizing flash of fire upward from my leg. Suddenly dizzy, I reached out to the far wall for support. At that moment a door which I now faced slid open. A well dressed man of smooth complexion and indeterminate age stood watching me.

For a second our eyes met and I felt the animosity of the man like a physical blow. A sense of revulsion filled me and I dropped my gaze to the floor. But I could still feel his look boring into me.

"Gentlemen," his voice was genial, "please come in. I've been expecting you."

My skin prickled. Suddenly I was afraid. Very deeply afraid.

"Trader Corbett," he went on, "you look as though you could use a chair. Allow me to welcome you to the School of Unification. My name is Saghy Garrison."

I stood, an hour later, on a level lower than Garrison's office, in an underground crypt beside a crystal stone that bore my brother's name, listening to Leader

107

Garrison extoll Ken's virtues.

"Your brother was a fine, sensitive man. His only mistake was in trusting the wrong people." Garrison's voice was suitably sympathetic. "He was only trying to help us—"

"But how—" My voice broke. Garrison's admission of Ken's death had come so suddenly after our earlier introduction that I still couldn't take it in. Garrison had brought me down here to the crypt to show me proof. "How did he die?" I'd been so certain—I touched the beautiful polished stone with Ken's name carved in. I'd been so *sure*—a black emptiness yawned in me.

"He was killed by an officer of the Brothers Security Force. We'd sent a team in to rescue him, but it was too late. All we got was his body."

"When did this happen?" Should I have come sooner? Would it have helped any if—

"Less than six weeks ago. Star-time, of course. You see, we knew where he was but we're a very poor group, and it takes money to mount that type of operation. We—is something wrong, Trader?"

I blinked, shaking my head. A chill shook me. Had I heard Garrison right? They were poor? Hovercars and Delta fields? Once more the hair was prickling on the back of my neck. I felt the smoothness of the crystal stone and struggled to keep my voice even. "Ken—" Garrison lied! *Ken was alive*. He had to be, or there'd be no sense to this charade. Feeling a hair's width from disaster, I drew a ragged breath. Remembering the hate I'd surprised in Garrison's eyes earlier, I knew now I had to convince him of my belief. "Nothing's wrong. I just—can I—can I take his body back to Illana? We have a family crypt there."

Garrison smiled the unctious smile of a burial attendant. "I'm sure that can be arranged." He took my arm and helped me toward the door past rows of the crystal stones. He nodded at the rows we passed. "As you can see, there've been many fallen heroes in the name of Unification."

A crystal graveyard. Diamonds for the dead. Garrison was right. Many had died, but not for the "cause" he espoused. More likely they were stones for buried monks who must have all had their ashes turned to dust due to his heresy.

But why was Garrison lying about Ken? And what could I do about it now? I needed time to think it out.

Telling me that we'd discuss the second part of my demand after he'd received some information he was expecting, Leader Garrison escorted me back through a rabbit's warren of halls and offices somewhere under the lecture hall. By the time we reached the room where Mike waited I knew we'd never get out on our own. How would we ever find our way?

Mike, folded into a chair reading Unification literature, looked up when I walked in, an angry frown on his face and something more. Worry? For me? Or worry that his quasi-prisoner might get away? That seemed more likely.

" 'Bout time you came back. I thought I'd have to pull down the Federation to find you."

"I'm not your concern, Pelonyi." And if I didn't need him right at the moment, I'd tell him where to go.

"You are until I have a chance to search your damned ship!"

Hadn't he already done that? Sinking down on the long lounge, I stuck a hard little pillow under my head and stretched out as best I could. God, I was tired. Damn Mike anyway. He sounded like a frequency-stuck space buoy. And there was no way to turn him off without saying more than I wanted Garrison and his group to hear. Because I could damned well bet we were bugged.

Mike tossed the papers to the low table beside his chair. "What are we waiting for?"

"The ship."

"Only the ship? What about your brother?"

"Ken's dead."

I felt Mike's sudden stillness. Then he cleared his throat. "I'm sorry."

"So am I."

Mike stood. His restless energy filled the room. "What makes you think they can get you the ship?"

I shaded my eyes from the bright overhead light panel and stared up at him. "Garrison said he'd see what he could do." I spoke as though I believed it. More probably Garrison was trying to figure out a way to get rid of Mike. But there was no way he could do that without bringing down massive Federation action. Federation didn't take kindly to losing its officers.

While I was still on that thought, the door opened and Beth entered with a tray. "We guessed you might be getting hungry. I brought fruit, cheese and wine." She cast me a sideways glance as though not sure how I'd react to her presence.

I waved her on to Mike. "Let Pelonyi have it. Federation food's so bad he needs all the help he can get."

Beth frowned. "Don't you feel well?"

"No," I said. "No, I don't. You see, this dumb lady I just happened to be married to went and shot me with a—"

Her tray hit the table with a clatter. Pale and shaking, she turned on me. "You don't have to joke about it. It was something I had to do, but I'm sorry—sorry that it happened. I really am."

"Oh, don't be. It's just one of those things. People

do it to each other all the time. Are you leaving?" I thought maybe it was my sarcasm that moved her so abruptly to the door, but she paused her hand on her hour badge.

"Yes, I'm due in the smaller lecture hall in fifteen minutes."

Smaller lecture hall? Mentally I tried to picture the size of the complex and what I conceived staggered my imagination. Good God, where was this group getting its backing?

Mike smiled at her, turning on his considerable charm. "Stay a moment, anyway, and tell us about Unification." He sounded like he really wanted to hear what she had to say.

Beth's face brightened. "It's Minder's hope for the future."

"Does your mother know that?" I said.

Beth shot me a contemptuous glance. "Unification is also the Brothers' only hope. Only then will—"

"Unified under who?" Mike interrupted. I thought he was egging her on but he looked only curious.

"Under a representative two-system government. That's the whole purpose behind the school. To teach the people who come how to rule. We don't have a lot of money," she paused smiling and I wondered how much she herself had put into it, "but we have plenty of enthusiasm and a marvelous leader. Saghy Garrison."

Again that prickly feeling crawled up my spine. But, staring at Beth, at her beautiful, guileless face, I knew she believed. And the belief was deep enough for her to act in a way which normally she might not. Suddenly I felt sorry for her. She was being used and didn't even know it.

Mike nodded as though he understood. Beth hesitated by the door. "Mr. Pelonyi—Mike—if I bring

111

back the dressing would you see to Gil's leg again?"

"You'll leave my damned leg alone!"

Mike ignored me. "Sure, Beth. Go get it. I'll hold him down if I have to." Beth nodded and quickly left.

"You and who else, Pelonyi?" I started to slide off the low couch but thought better of it. The world seemed steadier from a prone position.

"Nice girl," Mike said. He reached for a piece of fruit.

Sure she was. Covering my eyes again against the glare, I extended my sympathy to the Marquessa of Sandyminder. I bet she didn't believe in Unification either. Could she have any idea how deeply Beth was involved? No, or she'd have done something about it. The Marquessa didn't strike me as someone to sit back and see her world dissolve without trying to do something about it.

And this school? School of "Unification"?

What did they have to do with Silvernight and the propulsion pods and our experimental Class Fours?

The look in Garrison's eyes! I shivered. It still scared me.

Mike said, "Piece of fruit, Gil? I don't know what it is, but it smells good."

I turned to see if he was serious and he held up the orange ball as if to throw it to me. I shook my head. "Some people'll eat anything. That's a desert pear. Grows wild on the highlands."

He shrugged, took a bite and reached for the wine. I closed my eyes again. The world seemed more bearable that away.

Mike laughed softly. "Beth reminds me of Gardenia Blakemore."

Gardenia Blakemore? My mind reeled back several centuries. Cadet school. A class in Ancient History. Mike had been in love with her but so were we all.

That is, until we found out she thought Socrates and Hemlock were ships in the first Solar-Centuri race twelve hundred and some odd years ago. Socrates and Hemlock?

The poison cup? My lethargy vanishing, I darted a quick look at Mike. He held the wine to his nose as though appreciative of its bouquet I sighed. *Beth, dammit, how could you*? But by now I shouldn't be surprised, should I? "I see what you mean."

Mike chuckled. "I wonder whatever happened to Gardenia."

"She joined a Family Association out on Kaplan Two and had four kids and is now very rich."

"That figures." Putting the glass aside, Mike rose to his feet, seemingly filled with that restless energy he'd shown earlier. It took me only seconds to figure out what he was doing, as unobtrusively as possible. Searching for a monitor lens. I tried not to watch him.

Beth returned within minutes, a small med-kit under her arm. A shadow lay behind her smile. "Here it is, Mike, but I couldn't locate any daylon. Garrison gave me something else, though, and said it works just as well."

Anything Garrison recommended I certainly wouldn't take! But before I could say something to that effect Mike interrupted. "Thanks, Beth. Just leave the kit and I'll take care of him. Say, do you have time to have a glass of wine with me? Gil's not having any, and I hate to drink alone."

Beth didn't even hesitate. "All right, but only a little. I'm speaking to that group of students tonight, and I wouldn't want them to get the wrong impression of either me or the school."

Was she serious? I watched her. Did she really mean to drink?

Mike handed her the glass and she raised it to her

113

lips.

The sliding door caught us all by surprise. "Beth!" Min Balik's eyes were narrowly angry. "For God's sake, put that down and get up to the lecture hall. You're due to start in less than five minutes."

Annoyance flashed in Beth's face, but she laughed and laid the glass back on the small table by where Mike had been sitting. I met Mike's glance and knew what he thought. Min Balik herself had been monitoring us!

"Min Balik, please, could you help—" I pushed myself up, then fell back with a groan.

Immediately Beth was at my side. "Gil, what is it? What—"

Min Balik stepped into the room and Mike had her. Beth spun around, her face pale. "What are you doing?" She sounded like the autocrat of old.

Ignoring her, I rolled off the lounge and stood. My leg throbbed and briefly the room spun around me before it steadied. "Where's the camera Mike?"

Balik had been too surprised to struggle. Mike grinned at me from behind her dark head. "I've spotted two eyes. One in that vent," he nodded beyond me to a small grill high on the wall, "and another over the door."

With Beth watching me open-mouthed, I delved into the med-kit and found a tube of plastiskin. Now that Mike had pointed them out, I could see the lenses. Tiny things no bigger than rivet heads. I covered them both, and demanded from Beth, "Where's Garrison?"

"He's gone to—but—"

Min Balik recovered from her surprise. Angrily she twisted in Mike's arms but, of course, was no match for his strength.

But it was Beth who worried me most. The Marquessa expression was back in her face. "Gil, I won't

114

allow this."

"You want us dead instead?" Before Beth could decide to make a break for it, I moved closer to the door. Min Balik tore at Mike's arms with her nails, silently explosive.

Beth frowned. "Dead?" Suddenly she flushed. "Dead? Gil, that's crazy. No one wants you dead."

"Maybe not dead," I conceded. "Maybe just incapacitated."

"But Garrison said you wouldn't be hurt. He promised—"

"Shut up, Beth," spat Min Balik from Mike's arms. She had stopped struggling.

"Tell us what Garrison promised," Mike growled. "Was it that we'd deal?"

"Why, yes, of course." As though denying that any of this was happening, Beth shook her head. "Let Allia go. She's no threat to you." Edging toward the door, Beth watched us as though we were crazy men.

I moved again to block her. "Beth, what does Garrison want? Is it only the gold?"

"Of course. Ask Allia. She knows."

I wanted to laugh. Allia Balik probably knew a hell of a lot more than Beth did. Which might account for the touch of panic that had sprung to the Brothers woman's face.

But before I could warn Mike, Balik twisted in his arms so quickly he lost his grip. Instead of moving toward me and the door, she darted inward. In a split second I understood. "Mike! The wine!"

Mike moved before my words were barely spoken. Diving, he tackled Balik and brought her down just short of the small table where Beth had placed her glass. The table and glasses teetered. I held my breath. If we were ever to convince Beth, it'd have to be through the fact the wine was drugged.

115

Mike hauled Min Balik to her feet and pushed her away from the table toward the wall. Two long welts raised his cheek where she'd clawed him. His push wasn't gentle.

She turned on Beth. "If the wine's drugged, they've done it themselves."

Frightened, Beth looked at me.

I shook my head. "That's not true." I pointed up at the covered lenses. "Would Allia have come bursting in here to stop you from drinking if she hadn't known it was drugged?"

"I saw you put it in!" Balik spat.

"Which of us?" I demanded. "Me? Mike?"

Balik spoke without thinking. "You did it!" Her voice trembled with rage. "You!"

Confusion filled Beth's eyes.

Hauling Balik with him, Mike crossed the small room in three steps, grabbed one of the glasses and thrust it at the girl. "Drink it!"

Min Balik shook her head.

"What are you—" sputtered Beth.

"Beth," I asked, "did you pour the wine?"

"No. Garrison did before—"

Min Balik backed up until she hit the wall, still shaking her head. Mike advanced on her, holding out the glass. "You drink it, Min Balik, or I'll drown you in it." The fear in Balik's eyes grew real. I started to protest, but Mike had already grabbed her jaw, forcing her mouth open. She choked—and swallowed.

A long, breathless moment passed. Had we been wrong? Beth stared at her, mesmerized. Balik swayed and crumpled to the floor, out cold.

Mike sighed and I remembered to breathe.

Beth turned grey and sick-looking. "Is she—is she dead?"

Mike bent over and found a vein in the girl's neck.

"No."

My thoughts raced. How could we convince her? "Damn it, Beth, use your brain. Garrison wouldn't want to kill us. Not yet. He wants that gold."

"And," added Mike, "he wouldn't want a Federation murder charge messing up things."

Sure! He could always set it up later to make it appear I'd killed Mike! God, how *stupid* I'd been to think delivering the gold would be easy! "Beth," I went on, and it was no longer in me to be gentle with her, "Garrison is a liar, a dangerous and skillful liar. I don't know what part you play in all this, but you get in the way of my finding Ken and I'll kill you. Understand?"

Whether it was true or not, for the moment Beth seemed to believe me. Then she frowned. "Ken? But he's dead. Garrison said he'd died six months ago! He said you were foolish to believe—"

"That's strange. Garrison told me six weeks ago!"

"But Garrison said—"

"I don't give a damn what Garrison said!"

"Gil," Mike broke in, "don't argue with her. We've got to get out of here right now!"

Impatiently I nodded. He didn't have to tell me the obvious. But Beth—damn it, was she still unconvinced? Until she believed the truth, she'd be dangerous. To us—and to herself. Of course, we could put her out the way Mike had put out Min Balik. I started to say so, but Beth spoke, more to herself than to us. "But why? Why Saghy lie? He had no reason to lie to me."

"Beth!" Mike's voice cut like a whip. "Do you know who this man you call Garrison really is?"

"Of course I do." She turned eyes luminous with unshed tears on Mike. "He's the founder of the school here. I've known him for several years. And," her

117

chin lifted defiantly and her voice held renewed determination, "I trust him!"

"Did you know that he's been, for years, a representative of the Brothers System to other capitals of the Cluster? That he's one of the senior members of the Expansion Council? That he has the ear of the High Committee?" Mike's words made no sense to me, but they obviously did to Beth.

She paled and swayed, and caught the back of the chair. "No." Her voice dropped to a whisper. "It's not true. He can't be any of those things. Not Saghy Garrison." Bleakly she stared at Min Balik on the floor. It was as if she'd become suddenly numb to everything around her.

"Beth!" My sharpness made her look up to me. "Beth, get the med-kit and help me. I can't put plasti-skin on myself. And we've got to get out of here now!"

Beth nodded, but I could tell I still hadn't penetrated her shock.

Mike saw it too. A worried frown rode his face. "Beth, is there anywhere we can hide?"

She looked at him without comprehension.

Limping to her, I lifted her chin so that she had to see me, to hear me. Tears ran down her cheeks. "For someone," I said roughly, "who'll someday be Marquessa of Sandyminder, you certainly don't handle reality too well!"

She gasped and pulled away. Her face flushed angry red. Taking a deep breath, she glanced around as though seeing the room anew. "Let—let me look at your leg."

I sat heavily on the hard low couch, relieved that she seemed to have come back to us.

She talked as she worked. "There is another level. It's not used by the school except for storage. You can hide down there."

I hid a grimace. "How do we get there?"

"I think there's an entrance through the crypt."

I nodded. "I've been there. I can find it again." Maybe.

"I'll show you."

Mike had been pacing again. Now he stopped in front of us. "No—she'd better give her lecture, don't you think, Gil? She's safe as long as they don't suspect she knows what's really going on."

I didn't like the idea. I'd seen the hate at Garrison's core. If he suspected—

"I'm—" Beth's voice broke, and she tried again. "I'm safe enough. Many are here only because of me. I'll have to tell them—"

"God no!" I said. "Not yet!" I took her hand. It was a firm hand, but it trembled. I had a quick, hard fear for her. "Don't say anything yet."

"Why not? If what Mike says is true—" A touch of the autocrat returned to her demeanor "—then I've been an awful fool—"

"There's no sense in compounding one foolish act with another. You don't know how many people here are involved with Garrison. Don't take any chances!"

Watching me, a wild hope sprang to Beth's eyes. "If there's only a few, we could take over and throw them out!"

My heart sank. She actually meant it!

Impatiently Mike faced her. "Where in God's name are you, Beth?"

"Brother Timothy—" She stopped short and her face fell again. She was in perhaps the only place in the Cluster where she *wasn't* safe.

Mike touched my arm. "Ready?" I nodded. As ready as it was possible to be. "Check the door then. I'll bring Min Balik."

I agreed. We couldn't leave Balik where she might be found too soon.

Beth moved to the door ahead of me, still half dazed. My fear for her deepened. "How will you get out of here?" I asked.

"I come and go as I please." Tightly she grasped the side of the door. "But how can I go out there and say things I no longer believe?"

I took her shoulders, shook her gently. "You do believe. You believe in the idea of unity. You still believe in peace. You can still say so."

She smiled, but it was a poor replica of the real thing. "Be—be careful. I'll see what I can do about getting you back to your ship."

"No," I said. I'd be inclined to trust my own ability much more than hers. "We'll get out on our own. Just get yourself off Timothy as soon as possible without being too obvious about it."

Besides, having come this far I couldn't leave without locating Ken!"

As we slipped through the door into the empty hallway the last I saw of Beth was her haunted eyes.

10

I got lost twice on the way to the crypt, and once we were almost run down by a robocart winding its unattended way down one narrow passage.

"Garrison said how poor they were as an organization," I whispered, "yet they can afford hovercars and robocars and sophisticated monitoring equipment, can't they?"

We arrived at the open archway of the crystal crypt and I motioned him in. He passed by me and flopped Min Balik on a flat slab. "But where would they get that backing?"

"You said it yourself."

"The High Comittee?"

"How else would they've found out about the gold?" Because, obviously, now that I thought about it, Beth must have known long before I did. Long before our week on the — resolutely I put the thought out of my mind.

"You mean the whole thing was just one big con?"

"What do you think?"

Thoughtfully Mike nodded. "That'd explain a lot, but why steal the gold they've hired you to bring?"

Feeling like I was telling him something he already knew, I shrugged, "Because it wasn't the gold they wanted." No, it was the ship! But how had they found out about the Gabby? Who could've told them about her modifications? Ken? No, of course not. He hadn't known . . .

Mike shook his head, obviously puzzled. Did he expect me to tell him about Dunlevy's modifications? I searched for a good substitute answer. "Me."

"Why?"

I grinned. "Maybe they found out about Beth and me and thought I'd ruin their plans."

"And now they've got you."

He looked so damned serious I had to laugh. "Have they?"

His eyes full of unspoken speculation, Mike shook his head.

A few steps later we reached the rear of the large crypt, much further back than I'd been with Garrison, and there we found a low door, the one Beth had described. It looked unwieldy, but not particularly unused. Its handle was a sliding wheel lock of the type found in old inter-planetary passenger ships of three or four centuries ago. It'd been built into the rock of the back wall.

I tried the wheel but it refused to budge. "Clever old monks, weren't they, to cannibalize their ships for their hardware."

"One of the few thing we've seen that really looks monastic," Mike agreed. "Will it open?"

"Give me a hand."

Together we forced the wheel to move and the door opened on a flight of stairs going down. A curious low hum of distant machinery echoed in the silence. "Be careful," Mike said. He went back for Min Balik.

The third level below the School of Unification was a surprise. We'd expected darkness but light bars every twenty meters or so gave more illumination than we needed. Ahead the machinery sound became louder. The steps dropped us into a hall that was lined with cell-like rooms and at the first turn we almost ran into a group of uniformed guards. Brothers Security Forces!

We knelt in a shadowed recess and watched them go by.

Mike leaned close to my ear. "Security Service? What the hell are they doing down here?"

"How should I know?" I was beyond surprise. "Want to ask?"

Mike flashed a quick, hard grin. "Hell, no. I only want someplace to dump this hundredweight." He indicated Min Balik whose limp form rested still on his shoulder.

"Let me take her for awhile."

"No. I'm doing all right. Let's check this hall before someone else comes. Looks like another row of cells."

I nudged the nearest door open. Mike was right. The small room looked as though an ancient monk might have just stepped out. I nodded Mike fhrough and quietly closed the door behind us. A very small light source came on over the bare cot, another spotlighted a bare, dusty chest. "Austere," I whispered. "Early Federation I'd guess."

Mike lowered Min Balik to the cot with a grunt of relief, then moved back to the door. Gently he pulled out the old-fashioned lock. "Haven't seen locks like this since I left my grandmother's Family Association on Story IV."

"Great," I said, "if you know how to work it, let's get—"

A soft curse and the sound of someone falling outside the door whipped me around.

Strange how a certain kind of training never leaves you. Like Mike, I moved before I reasoned it out. We flattened ourselves against each side of the partially-opened door and for the second time in thirty hours I cursed my lack of a weapon.

The door swung wide. "Dump'm here 'til we got one down to ident'm," mumbled someone out of my line of sight.

"One of that damned Minder bunch, I'll o—"

The guard backing in saw me but before he could do anything more Mike lifted the LEM from his belt. "Bring him right on in, men, this is the proper place."

The Brothers guards were completely engaged with a limp form between them and were in no position to argue. Tight-faced, they did as Mike said.

I lifted the second guard's LEM, caught Mike's eye and touched my hour badge. He glanced at the guards again and noticed what I'd already seen. Each carried communicators instead of hour badges around their necks. He nodded, silently pointing at the floor. The two men, after glancing at each other and then at their misplaced LEMs, put their burden down.

"Turn around. Against the wall." Mike's voice was soft but there was nothing soft in his face. He ripped the communicators from each man's neck and handed them to me. I sought a place to hide them, and finally shoved them under Min Balik on the hard cot. Then I went to the man on the floor, knelt and turned him over.

I knew him, damn it, but—of course! Des Filemon! The kid who'd followed Ken all over Sandy. But what was he doing here?

He stirred and opened his eyes. Focused on me. His hand went to the back of his neck and a hard, angry protest formed on his face. He struggled to sit up. "What the—"

I offered him a hand and pulled him to his feet. "We didn't do it," I said. "They did." I pointed to the two guards. Confusion replaced his anger. I went on. "Are you all right? Can you walk?"

The young man still rubbed the back of his neck. "I—I think so." He sounded functioning.

"Gil—" Mike tapped his hour badge. I nodded.

Federation teaches her men many things. I don't approve of most, but I have to admit they're effective.

With a quick chop of his open hand Mike put each guard out. He knew what I was thinking and grinned. Which is why he's the soldier and I'm the trader.

I touched Des Filemon on the arm and motioned him to follow. Time enough to question him later when we'd found a hiding place.

We found our place, an old storage area with a layer of dust on its empty shelves that said it hadn't been used for years. I made the introductions.

Mike didn't like this addition to our equation one little bit. "What are you doing here?" He sounded barely civil.

Des hesitated and I wondered if we'd get the truth or a handy fabrication. But then he lifted his shoulders as if to say it really didn't matter. "The other night when I left your ship on Sandy, there were two men—"

I remembered the pair who'd done the damage on the Gabby and nodded. The ones who'd hit me with that little handheld laser.

"—lying outside the perimeter of your field seal, watching. I pretended I didn't see them, but I came back a few minutes later." He smiled slightly. "They didn't see me that time. I took a good picture with the night-cam. One was a guy I saw with Silvernight while your brother was on Sandy. I felt they were more important than going to work, so I followed them back here." He sank down on his heels and leaned against the cold rock wall. He looked tired. "We got here a

125

couple of hours ago.''

Mike stared down at him, hard-faced, doubting. "When did you leave Sandyminder?"

Des Filemon looked at his hour badge. "Two and a half days ago . . Star-time."

They'd had a faster trip than we'd had. "How did you do it? How did you follow them?"

He smiled. "I went aboard their ship with a few boxes."

My respect for him grew.

But Mike grunted. "You mean you stowed away?"

"Yeah," said Des. "What of it?"

I grinned. "Stop being a Service Man, Mike. It happens all the time." I turned back to Des. "Just ignore him. Born obnoxious. What kind of a ship did you come on?" The 'Bella, maybe?

"It's a Five, almost as big as a Federation ship."

A big Five. That figured, given everything else Class-A about this operation. But I couldn't help my disappointment. What had they done with the Bella? Surely they couldn't hide her. They'd have to bring her out sometime. Then something else occurred to me. "Des, what were you doing outside that particular door? The one where the guards found you?"

For the first time Des Filemon appeared uncertain. "I-I was following you."

Mike tensed. Glanced at me. "Where did you pick us up?"

"Up there by the door to that crystal room—"

"You mean the crypt?"

"Yeah." Des shifted uneasily. "I recognized the trader here. Wanted to know what you were doing." His eyes shadowed. "Where's Beth?"

"Upstairs." I hoped she still was.

"Is she all right?"

I hoped that, too. "For the time being." My thoughts

126

went back to the 'Bella. "Des, have you seen another Class Four around here? Like mine?"

"You mean your brother's? Not since he left Sandy."

Hell! The trail was too cold. We'd never find it! What if Mike was right? What if they'd already—

Mike picked up on my thought. "With Silvernight around, it's possible they did break her up, Gil."

Dunn's propulsion pods—would Silvernight know what he had? Of course! And he had been on Sandy— and I was right back where I started. My head suddenly throbbing, I leaned against the wall and rubbed my face. A vicious, damned merry-go-round! "If they broke her up, then I've gotten us into one hell of a mess for nothing!"

"No." Mike frowned thoughtfully. "Not for nothing. Looks like we've uncovered something more important here than the 'Bella. This School of Unification, for instance—"

"Maybe for you, Mike, but we had everything we owned tied up in that ship and her experimental pods."

"What experimental pods?"

A stillness grew in me. I was afraid to look at him. He knew! Why did he pretend not to? "It doesn't matter now." I turned back to Des. "Do you know the way out?"

"I know the way I came in. A freight belt."

"Can we get out that way?"

"Guess so."

"Good." Looking at the dust-layered floor, I suddenly knew if I didn't lie down I'd fall. "When—things quiet out there, we'll leave."

"Not without Beth—" Des began.

"With or without her," I said harshly.

In my dream the 'Bella wa a bright star on the scope and even as I watched she exploded. A huge predatory

127

bird came and ate the pieces and each piece was a piece of me, and the predatory bird said his name was Silvernight. I awoke in an icy sweat with Mike shaking me.

"A new shift is on, Gil. I think we'd better get out while we can."

I struggled to stand but my leg wouldn't hold me. Panicked, I pulled myself up against the wall, choking on the smell of ancient dust. Resting against the rougher rock of the wall I tried to work some feeling into my numb leg. How in the hell could I get out if I couldn't walk?

Mike offered his hand. "Lean on me."

"He won't make it up that freight belt!" Des, standing by the cracked door was looking back at us over his shoulder.

I pushed Mike away. "I can do it by myself." Suddenly my stomach lurched. Beth! Was she all right? Then anger rolled over me. What if she wasn't? What did I care? She'd used me the way she herself had been used. How did she like the feeling?

For a long time Mike studied me, waiting I supposed for me to fall, but when I didn't he moved to the door beside Des and peered out. "Which way from here, kid?"

"Down this hall and to the right. But I tell you, it's a hard climb. The trader won't make it."

I agreed. My leg throbbing harder with every pulsing heartbeat, I had to agree. I could no more climb a freight belt than I could fly without jets. "I'll go out the way we came in."

Mike faced me squarely. "I'm not leaving you behind, Gil."

"For God's sake, Mike, you have to. Listen, you've got to get back to the Gabby. I don't want the Brothers to claim her!"

"They won't do that with the Eagle standing by—"

"They might try. Mike—" A cold knot grew in my stomach. A certainty that I knew what I had to do. That I had no other choice. "Promise me—"

Mike's eyes grew dark. "What?"

"Promise that if I don't get there by Morning Ten star-time you'll take the Gabby out to the limit and blow her core!"

Mike's eyes widened in protest. "But—"

"Morning Ten, Mike. Promise me."

Mike's jaw worked. He hesitated. Finally nodded. "All right. But if you aren't out by Morning Nine, I'll bring down Federation to find you!"

11

After Mike and Des had gone, I leaned against the door listening. Would I hear the shouts if they were discovered?

I'd given Des the second LEM we'd lifted from the guards, which made Mike even angrier than he was at my decision to remain behind. But I didn't care how angry he got as long as he agreed to do what I wanted. Blow the Gabby's core!

Gathering my strength, I knew the truth. It was now or—I slipped through the door into the long, bright hall.

Immediately I felt exposed. And each step was a more painful reminder that Mike was probably right. I couldn't make it. But damn it, I had to try!

Coming to the first corner I became momentarily confused. To my right a passageway led into a large open area filled with boxes and crates. That had to be the way to the freight belt Des had come down.

Straight ahead the passageway went fifty meters and turned. The one to my left led to a glass-enclosed jumpchute. Its metal work was shiny and clean. New. Certainly not something the old monks would've thought of. Add that to the list of things this outfit shouldn't have been able to afford!

Staring at it, an idea sprang to mind. Of course! The

perfect way out! Especially if it went all the way to the surface!

But what if someone came down just as I was—

Go back to the crypt?

No, no way I could find my way back through this maze of halls to that crystal room. The jumpchute would have to be it!

Nervously I moved along the hallway toward the brightly lit booth, past two dark doorways that stood open on my right, past a third that was shut tight. I almost reached a fourth when the jumpchute clanged and hissed. Someone coming down!

Stumbling in haste, I fell toward the fourth doorway. Open! Dark—just enough light shown from the hall to reveal a desk, a chair, shelves of simex book tapes, and a reading unit with a light-comp drawing plate and fingerbar. I touched the reading unit. It was cold, and the light-comp—warm! Someone had been working in here just a short time before. Were they coming back?

Voices from the jumpchute. Loud, sharp, protesting. I moved to the doorway and flattened myself along one side. A male voice, querulous and petulant. "You can't do this! You promised. That was one of the conditions!"

Silvernight! It had to be.

"With a Federation vessel in Parking Orbit, Professor? If you had any sense—" A door sighed and the voice cut off, but I'd heard enough to recognize Edward Randall White himself! Then the hiss of the door again. "Drink your tea and go to sleep, Professor. I'll be back to let you out in the morning."

Like a pet—or a prisoner.

No, damn it, I couldn't jump to conclusions. It probably wasn't that way at all. He was here, like Beth, because he wanted to be. But I shuddered to think what the Brothers could do to the rest of us with the knowledge that was in that old man's head!

I edged to the doorway again and saw White re-entering the jumpchute. The clang of metal, the hiss and the spring, and he was gone again.

Hidden in my safe doorway, I studied the doors across the way.

Four, matching those on this side. All closed. Which hid Silvernight? Did I really want to know?

Yes, Silvernight knew about Ken! He must! He was the link!

I limped out to check the doors opposite but again the jumpchute hissed. I glanced down that way and my heart hammered. Garrison! Shaking, I ducked back into the dark room.

Hard, fast footsteps pounded down the hallway. I sank deeper into the shadows. Had they seen me? God, *had they?*

Garrison, angry. "Which way?"

"Corridor 14, Room 6, I think she said."

"How did they get down here? How much did Allia have? How in the hell did you let—"

They pounded by, and I held my breath. Min Allia Balik was awake? The whole place would soon be in an uproar.

The moment they turned the corner at the end of the block of cells I was across the hall. No time for subtleties. I had to find Silvernight.

All the doors had the old mechanical locks. Saving my leg as much as I could I ran back and jerked the fingerbar from the drawing board. With a loud metallic screech it tore loose. I ran back into the hall.

The lock on the first door gave quickly and the door slid open with a bang. A man sat up on the bed. "What do you want?"

His face tugged at my memory, but I couldn't put a

name to him, "Are you all right, sir?"

"Of course I am. What's all the commotion tonight?"

I forced a smile. "No problem. A couple of strangers broke in and we're looking for them."

"Need any help?"

"No, thanks." I backed out and heard him slide an inside lock. My heart hammered in my ears. The encounter had taken mere seconds but it seemed like forever. My leg throbbed with the regularity of a big bass drum.

Ignoring it as best I could, I went on, but I had the niggling feeling I should have known who the man was. That somehow it was important. But Silvernight was my only interest now. All I had time for.

The fingerbar broke on the next lock but the lock came loose and the door opened. Silvernight sat on the edge of his bed holding a cup with both hands. He looked up. Petulance gave him the air of an unhappy child.

"What now?" he grumbled. Then peered at me. The cup trembled. "Corbett?"

"Sh!" I pointed to the open door, indicating the way out. But how did he know who I was? The cup clattered when he laid it on the table I mouthed the word hurry, and he nodded.

When he reached the door I whispered, "Who's in that other room?" I pointed to the one I'd just left.

"Patterson Reed."

An electric fear shot through me. "The weapons man?"

Silvernight nodded.

"How about these others?" I nodded at the other two closed doors. How many more experts did Garrison have down here?

"The Sandyminder girl's in the next one."

133

I was too numb for surprise. We were only two doors from the jumpchute now. I used the light bar again and the lock opened.

In the middle of the room Beth, on her feet and frightened, nonetheless stood with a leg from the bedside table raised in her hands ready to clobber whoever stepped through the door. She dropped it when she saw me. "Oh, Gil! Thank God. I thought—"

"Never mind. They've found Min Balik. We've got to get out of here."

"Where's Mike?"

"Already gone."

She caught sight of Silvernight. "Lorcas?"

"Silvernight." I pushed her toward the jumpchute. "Come on!"

"But Mike—where—"

"No time to explain. Get in there!" I pushed her into the jumpchute. Silvernight crowded in behind. "Does this thing go all the way to the surface?"

"No—" began Beth.

"Yes," said Silvernight.

I pulled the door shut behind us. Silvernight probably knew more than Beth did. But then I caught sight of the last door I hadn't opened. A thought jumped at me. Ken's? I grabbed Silvernight's collar. "That last room. Who's in there?"

"No one, now."

The way Silvernight said it made me take a closer look at him. His kindly eyes were somewhat befuddled. But what had I heard in his voice?

"Who was—"

"Your brother, the trader Corbett."

Ken—I broke out in a sweat. "Where is he now?"

"They moved him out to the ship this morning."

But why—Beth grabbed my arm. "They're coming back—"

Hard boots pounded on the tile. "I hear them. Where's the damned control on this thing?"

"They're all right there," said Silvernight calmly.

I spun on him, furious. "Can you get us to surface?"

"Can you get me off this infernal planet?"

"I can—"

Silvernight reached around me and flipped open the control box, punched a hidden button and we shot upward.

"The students weren't allowed to use it," Beth said. I caught the apology in her voice. She hadn't known how to run it either.

Lighted levels alternated with dark and passed so quickly they made me dizzy. I held on and shut my eyes. Ken! God, to be so close! "Where did they take him, did you say?"

"The ship. Your ship."

"My ship?"

"No, the other one. The one you call the Arabella. They've renamed her, naturally. They call her 'Monks Retreat.'"

"But that's—" Beth started, then looked at me with eyes wide with disbelief.

"The ship," I finished for her, "that you were to fly triumphantly home in? You and all your peaceful, conquering heroes?"

Silvernight snorted. "They've made the Monk's Retreat into a first class little warship. If I'd known what you were using in her pods for fuel they'd have launched an attack on Minder four or five weeks ago."

About the time, I thought, that Balik found Beth and I were married.

The jumpchute slid to a stop. I motioned the others out, took the small piece of fingerbar that I had left

135

and smashed the control until sparks flew. The lights flickered out. They wouldn't come after us that way!

Stepping from the jumpchute I came to a stop. We were at the very back of the large lecture hall behind the last tier of seats.

"Hey, Beth—" My soft voice made feathery echoes down the tiers. Beth turned and I pointed to the far side. "Isn't that where we came in?"

"Yes."

"Is that door open? Can we get out that way?"

"I don't see why not."

I could think of several reasons why not, the greatest of which was Leader Garrison, three or four levels below.

Garrison!

As though I'd conjured his form from black smoke, Garrison sprang to three-dimensional life in front of the enlarger screen at the bottom of the hall. Larger than life. Growing. Evil!

"Ah, Captain Corbett, we know you're up there. You can't get away, you know. Even if you leave the complex, there's nowhere to go."

His smile was gentle, chilling.

Beth stood staring, transfixed. "Come on," I whispered. Silvernight had already moved across the back row toward the far door.

Garrison's voice followed us. "You're injured, Corbett. You need help. We can help you."

There was no shutting him off. And with every step I took, I knew he was right. I stumbled, half fell. I heard Beth gasp.

"Go on," I shouted. "Don't stop!"

I reached the door after the other two were through and turned for one last look at the super-life-sized image. Caught my breath. He seemed to be staring at *me*. Laughing at our efforts! I passed through the door, slammed it behind me, shutting off the sight and sound.

I stood, trembling against the door, in inky darkness. What was it about the man that made me so afraid?

Slowly my eyes grew accustomed to the dark. Above the stars shone, one extremely bright. Minder. Ahead I could see the staired pathway we'd come by. The one Beth had led me down so many hours ago. I caught up with them and Beth turned to start upward. I stopped her. "Beth, wait. How long has Garrison known we were gone? Are there guards out there?"

Beth shook her head. "I—don't know. I told him Allia had taken you two off somewhere. I didn't tell him—I only accused him—" she shuddered. "He's horrible. Absolutely horrible. How could I have been so blind—so—"

Grabbing her shoulders I shook her hard enough to rattle her teeth and stop her rising hysteria. "How did you get caught?"

"I accused him—of—of using me—"

She would, I thought. She was just dumb enough. "What did he—" She laughed but it held the sound of tears. "He was furious. Especially at our being married. He hadn't known. They were afraid to tell him—" She started to laugh again, and I gave her another emphatic shake. She jerked away from me.

"You mean our getting married wasn't Garrison's idea?" A sudden lightness touched my thoughts then fled again. What did it matter whose idea it was? It was all wrong anyway. I looked up again at the sky, at the star that cast its glow. The rocky hills were blacker shadows against the purple black sky. Black as our chanced of escaping. Black as Beth's chances of ever seeing Minder again!

"How could I," Beth continued softly, "how could I

have been so stupid?" Tears colored her voice. Quickly she turned from me and started upward following Silvernight who had already started the climb.

My last shred of patience fled. I followed her. "I don't know, damn it. How could you? I've seen some stupid people in my day, but you really beat them all!"

Beth stopped abruptly and I ran into her. "And damn it," I added, "don't stop. I'll fall over you."

She climbed again, faster, and I thought I heard Silvernight chuckle in the gloom ahead.

Silvernight and Beth reached the top of the path ahead of me and rested on the flat rocks. I fell down beside them and reached for another daylon capsule but found only an empty pocket. A hollow uneasiness rode me. A feeling of helplessness. Was Garrison right? Would I not make it? No, I thought. I *had* to make it.

From what I could see by the faint starlight, we rested in a natural saddle on a high ridge with what appeared to be the ruins of old buildings on the side we'd just climbed. On the other side a series of sharp hills fell to an alluvial plain several kilometers away.

The shiny surface of a car path wound its way upward through the hills, stopping some way below us. It didn't look too far away to reach in a reasonable period of time. Maybe we'd make it out after all. Sure we would!

"Gil, there's an air car down there. See? We can use it!"

"Where?" I turned to where she pointed and saw it too. I could also see something else. The shine of starglow on something that moved. "You two wait here. I'll take a look."

"Gil," said Beth, "Garrison was right when he said you couldn't go much farther on that leg. Let me go."

And do what? Get us caught? "Beth, you move one eyelash when I tell you not to and I'll smack you silly."

Beth spun to face me. Her voice rose. "You're insufferable, Gil Corbett! If you think—"

"And if you don't shut up," I continued, "the whole system will know exactly where we are!" As if they didn't already. But at least we had a little head start.

Abruptly Beth sat. I didn't need to see clearly to feel the heat of her stark anger.

Silvernight chuckled again. "He's right, girl. Let him handle it."

What Beth muttered under her breath I didn't ask her to repeat.

Turning my attention to the shadows and rocks, I followed the path down to the clearing some way below. Where the hovercar sat. With the Brothers security guard leaning casually against it.

He made a perfect target. Too perfect. Either they wanted us to take him and escape in the hovercar—or they would catch us when we tried.

Quietly I backed off and returned the way I'd come.

Beth gasped when I fell down beside her for the second time. "You scared me! I didn't hear you come—"

"You weren't supposed to," I said. "It's a setup down there. We'll have to find another way."

"Gil—" Beth grabbed my arm and pointed down the school entrance. Lights flashed on, flooding the bottom of the stairway. Ten security guards, a unit, in black and red and very official looking uniforms marched through the door and started up the staired pathway.

But coming from the light that way, I knew they hadn't seen us yet. "Come on," I whispered. "Let's get out of here."

We climbed higher in the rocks. The way I figured it, the old monks wouldn't have isolated themselves with only one way out. Surely they'd have left themselves another way—but by the time we found it— Time! A

139

sinking sensation hit the pit of my stomach. I stopped abruptly to look at my hour badge.

Beth stopped behind me and Silvernight came into view.

"Beth, what time is it surface?"

"Oh, Gil, I don't know. Late. Why?"

"Because it's Morning Four, star-time." And at Morning Ten—I couldn't finish the thought. But what if Mike and Des hadn't made it out of the complex? Or were holed up somewhere?

"Are you all right, Gil?" Beth sounded concerned. It struck me as funny.

"Yes."

I found another trail shortly after, and it, too, wound down toward the car path. It was more precipitous and much more tiring than the climb up the other path had been and it took us much longer. Almost forty-five minutes by my hour badge. We came out below a roadblock of sorts. I started to breathe a little easier.

Then I saw him. The guard reflected starshine. His back was partly to us and he looked up the car path. This was no decoy. Starshine also glistened off the LEM at his belt.

Damn it, I wanted that LEM. I already regretted giving mine to Des. I was tired of being unarmed. I pointed the guard out to Beth and Silvernight. "Wait here."

"Your young man," Silvernight said to Beth, "is a man of many talents."

"He's not my young man!" Beth raised her voice and the guard tensed and half turned, looking for the sound. Damn them anyway! Why couldn't they shut up! I held my breath, waiting for him to move again. When he did; I covered the remaining distance with a speed that brought fiery pain to my leg but gave me a brief and accurate savagery. I connected with his neck and he fell without a struggle. Mike would've been proud of me.

But when I bent over the guard's limp form to retrieve the LEM from his belt, a surge of revulsion gagged me. Violence had never been my style. Another reason I'd not been a successful Federation Service Man.

Beth ran up with Silvernight close behind. "You killed him!"

"I doubt it." I tucked the LEM in my belt and turned away.

"He'll die if you leave him here."

I doubted that too.

"Gil—" Beth's voice carried a harsh, warning note.

I spun on her. "You don't care who you hurt, but you don't want me to hurt anyone, is that is?"

Beth became very quiet.

I started down the car path, little caring whether or not they followed.

The car path wound down the mountainside and afforded us a spectacular view of the distant city. the strings of light spread out along the street lines like tentacles on a meridian lion-dog. Some spread in our direction. We could even make out the lighted outlines of the shuttle field on the far side of the city. The far side. We still had a long way to go.

Halfway down the mountain, still travelling on the car path, Beth said, "Gil, there's a car below us."

I'd also just spotted it. "With lights. I see it. Get into the rocks. And stay down!"

I watched the hovercar. It was a huge, malevolent bug walking on legs of light, stabbing light fingers into the dark and waving antennae of lights at the rocks above us.

When they went by I counted six security men and a driver. Then they disappeared around the next hairpin turn. Beth stood.

"Don't move!" I whispered.

She dropped back into position. "But why?"

"Thermograph."

"A what?"

"He means, girl," said Silvernight, "that they've taken a heat picture of the area as they've passed. If they come back, taking another to compare, they'll see immediately where we've been."

"When will they come back?"

"How the hell—" I stopped as suddenly as I began. It did no good to vent my frustration on Beth. Too late now for anger. I leaned my head against the rock. Felt it cool under my cheek. God, I was tired. I closed my eyes.

"Gil! Gil! Listen. It's coming back!"

I awoke with a jerk. The hovercar lit the rocks above us with light. I sank down closer to the ground and prayed the others did the same. The hovercar stalked past and disappeared.

We waited until the sound was gone then waited until I was sure they'd not stopped somewhere just below.

Beth finally stirred. "Are they gone for good?"

"For now."

"Do we have to stay here?"

"No. We'll go on."

"Gil—" Beth's voice dropped to a whisper. "I-I'm scared."

It was a tremendous admission on her part but I couldn't be overly sympathetic. "Good! Just make sure you stay that way!" I felt no contrition for being harsh. Not now. Maybe later—if there was a later.

We stopped again when my hour badge read Morning Five-thirty, and only then because I simply couldn't go on any further. The city and shuttle field looked no closer than they had before but we were almost off the mountain. The plains stretched out before us.

Silvernight agreed to the halt. "I have to rest. Not as young as I once was."

"Are any of us?" Beth said.

I dropped to the hard rocky ground and pulled my jacket off. The world had a tendency to spin. I looked up at the stars. Minder was no longer apparent and the others blurred together like grains of sand on the beach. I shut my eyes. We couldn't make it back to the Gabby in time. God, if only Mike did it, if only he blew the core, and blew the gold to sparkling bits of dust—the fuel too. Dunn's fuel that he hoped someday would take us back to civilization—someday. How did he know there was any civilization to go back to? What if we were a thousand years too late? "Too late," I muttered.

Beth knelt beside me. I felt her presence and smiled. "Not a very nice honeymoon, is it?"

"Gil, you're burning—"

"No, the air's turned cold." I opened my eyes but her face was only a shadow against the lighter sky. I looked to the stars beyond.

They winked and moved and spun. Dizzily I shut my eyes again. Beth's hand was icy on my forehead. "You should've brought a jacket, Beth. You'll be cold before dawn."

A short time later I opened my eyes again. I thought I'd heard something, but I wasn't sure what. This time the stars stood still. At least the ones I could see. See?

That shadow! I grabbed for the LEM at my belt. That was a shuttle out there blocking the stars! A space shuttle! I struggled up fumbling with the LEM. The shuttle was moving lower . . .

Federation, by the size—

Beth grabbed my arm. "Gil, you're crazy. What are you trying to do?"

I couldn't spare the energy to answer. Pushing her away, I tried to remember—so long ago. Each cadet had a special code. Mike's had been Pillow. Mine was—what? Corbett—Orbit? Odd that I could remember Mike's before I could my own!

I used the LEM to blink the code-light Orbit, again and again. The lights of the shuttle came closer. Had it seen us yet?

Silvernight came to his feet pointing back at the mountain. "There's that hovercar again. It's leaving the road."

"Gil, they've seen us. The hovercar sees us!"

Suddenly I heard the soft roar of the shuttle's thrusters. Fire appeared beneath her as she swung around and settled between us and the Brothers hovercar.

Mike's voice roared above the sound of the thrusters. "Hurry, damn it, they're right on our tail!"

"You heard the man!" I shoved Beth toward the shuttle. "Get moving!"

She ran, with Silvernight close behind. I watched with relief. Relief. But it all seemed very remote. I wasn't a part of it. Then I was back on that cool rock again, tasting the ancient dirt of Brother Timothy. So very tired. Then nothing.

12

I awoke to a cold ice pad on my forehead. "Shades of my grandmother Dorrie," I grumbled, "whatever happened to modern doctoring?" I tried to move but seemed curiously weighted down.

"You've had that, too." Beth's voice was soft, quieting. I pulled the cloth off. I was home. The main sleeper of the Gabby. The room I'd turned over to Beth. Someone had stripped me and put me to bed. Plastiskin encased my whole left leg and my mouth was curiously numb as though I'd ingested a strong drug. I wore something that could only have come from the destitute imagination of a Federation clerk! What every well-dressed dead man wears to the wake. I tried to lift my head off the pillow but my muscles wouldn't work. Falling back, I reached for my hour badge but it wasn't around my neck. Frustration washed over me. "What time is it?"

Beth handed me my small silver tri-timer. "27:45. How do you feel?"

"Alive." Barely. I struggled again to sit up but then thought better of it. The action seemed to take more effort than I really wanted to make. Sudden memory of recent past events washed over me. "Where's Pelonyi?"

"Mike's in the lounge reading."

"You're kidding. He can't read." An urgent need to know what in the hell was happening welled up in me. I raised my voice. "Pelonyi?"

He appeared in the doorway, a relieved expression on his face. "What's the matter?"

"How do we sit?" I shut my eyes to listen.

"We've got the gold, they've got the 'Bella and Ken. They want you and the gold. They've appealed to the Federation. Federation says it's none of their business." He chuckled softly. "They're getting nervous."

"Why?"

"Because they haven't heard from you in four days."

"Four—" I jerked alert, staring at him. Four days? Was he joking? No. "Well, hell!" And delivery date on the gold was—was yesterday if I hadn't lost count. "Ten thousand credits for every day we sit here now."

Beth's eyes shadowed. "Can they make you pay it?"

"It's in the contract." I thought of something else. "Why do they want me, Mike? Kidnapping Silvernight?"

"Don't know. Anyway, Silvernight says he won't go back."

"Where is he?"

"Over on the Eagle."

I closed my eyes again. The desire for sleep washed over me in waves. But I smiled. At least they admitted they held Ken and he was still alive. Right now that was the only concern. Ken was still alive!

I awoke again six hours later to voices drifting in from the lounge. "—leave when your Eagle leaves, Mike!" Beth. A weak sadness filled me. I didn't want her to leave.

Mike said, "I'm no nursemaid, Beth. Gil needs

146

you."

"Gil doesn't need anyone. Not as long as he has the Gabby."

"The Gabby can't take care of him now."

"He'll be up tomorrow. The doctor said so."

That was nice to know. And if she wanted to leave, fine. Let her. What did I care!

I shut my eyes again but this time I didn't go back to sleep. How was Pete? Had there been any word from Illana? When was the Federation ship leaving? Where was the Bella now? The Monk's Retreat—not a very nice name for such a pretty lady. But then, she was no lady anymore, not if they'd armed her.

Patterson Reed, weapons expert. Silvernight, fuel expert. What a combination. Restlessness attacked me. What were they doing? I had to get of this bed and find out! "Mike?"

He came to the door, a question on his face.

"Help me get out of this damned bed, will you?"

"Why?"

"I want to talk to Silvernight."

"I told you he's not here. He's over on the Eagle."

"Oh." Had he told me? I couldn't remember. "When do you leave?"

"Eagle leaves tomorrow at Morning Two. But I think I'll stick around. Looks like things'll get interesting."

"Who invited you?" My anger came back full force. Mike couldn't make that decision on his own. No way. His orders came from his Captain who in turn got them from Federation Control. "Am I still being investigated on the DTC charge?"

Mike frowned. "Among other things."

I fumed, but—better to let him come than end up in the Eagle's brig myself!

Silvernight came aboard three hours later, once

more the wild-haired, diffident genius professor. But he didn't fool me now. On the way down that mountain he'd had complete control of his faculties. His absentminded professor bit might be a good mask, but I'd seen behind it and he wouldn't fool me again.

"Don't understand it. I just don't. They wouldn't let me take a look at your fuel pods. I just wanted to look."

I watched him from my recliner in the lounge. Mike, leaning against the galley door in his favorite pose of nonchalance, watched us both.

"The pods wouldn't tell you anything," I said finally. "The difference is in the fuel itself."

Silvernight scowled, but I had the impression I'd surprised him. "You couldn't possibly get that KKS from a change of fuel!"

Mike straightened, but I ignored him. "Silvernight, how did you find out about the KKS?"

A shrewd expression passed behind the old man's eyes. "In the very distant past we had those speeds. They brought us from the furthest reaches of the galaxy. Distances beyond imagination. Do you have any idea what we could do if we had those speeds now?"

I could imagine what would happen to the rest of us if the Brothers had that speed and no one else did. "You haven't answered my question."

"Oh—" A wave of his hand dismissed my concern, "—an accident."

"What kind of an accident?"

Looking uncomfortable, Silvernight squirmed in his seat. Before our eyes he once more became just a befuddled old man. "Hounding, hounding," he muttered, "forever hounding me. You want my secrets," he tapped his head and grinned slyly, "but they're all safe. Safe right here."

I said a dirty word and closed my eyes.

"I guess he doesn't really want to see those fuel pods after all," said Mike.

Silvernight froze. Yes, yes indeed he did. More than anything else in the universe, obviously, he wanted to see the Gabby's pods!

I sighed and tipped the recliner forward. "Get him out of here. Senile old bastard! I'm going back to bed."

Silvernight jumped up. "Wait!" Neither his voice nor his hand trembled. "I'll tell you. Let me see the pods and I'll tell you."

"Tell us first," said Mike.

Silvernight told us, in words that didn't falter once, how three armed Brothers Class Five warships had attacked a single trader, the Arabella, Class Four, out of Illana. They'd expected, at most, token resistance. The 'Bella was outclassed, outarmed and had no way to run. Or so they thought.

But as soon as Ken realized what was happening he'd kicked in the experimental pods and run for Sandyminder, which was his next stop anyway. And who'd notice if he arrived early? But the Class Fives followed him, followed the faint ionization that was his trail.

My mind went off on a tangent. Damn it, how had she handled, using Dunn's pods? I'd thought it'd be dangerous at high speed. She wasn't built for a continuous high stress. But Ken and Dunn thought otherwise. Which of us was right? Did the rods fire as long as we thought they would? What speed had she attained? Had it all happened too fast or had Ken managed to record her fantastic flight?

Questions only Ken could answer.

"Well?" Silvernight demanded.

"Well what?" I hadn't heard him stop talking.

"Do I get to see the pods?"

149

"One more question first. How did you get Ken to go on to the Brothers?"

"The School of Unification. I came to him personally and asked for his help in delivering supplies to the school."

Mike threw out his hands. "And the idiot bit! God, you Corbetts would fall for any line anyone handed you!"

I bristled at Mike's tone. But maybe Ken hadn't been so wrong at that. The best way to hide something is to pretend you have nothing to hide. Maybe—it was a possibility—by the time Ken reached Sandy he had nothing left. He'd put on a tremendous burst of speed. He probably had to kick in all the auxiliary pods at once. Maybe by the time he reached Sandy the fuel was gone. In fact, it had to be, if Silvernight was here asking to see the Gabby's pods. If one drum had been left unused, Silvernight wouldn't be here now!

Suddenly feeling good, I grinned at Mike. "Take Silvernight back and show him the fuel."

With a look of protest, Mike stiffened. "I don't think he should be allowed—"

"No reason not to." I watched Silvernight to see how he'd take this. "All the Gabby carries is standard Class Four pods with Standard Dunlevy fuel."

Silvernight flushed. He leaned forward, every muscle strained with rage. "You lied to me! You lied!"

"You assumed," I replied. I was suddenly very, very tired.

Beth came back from the Eagle at Evening One, 21:00 hours and punched in a big evening meal for the three of us that my stomach said was long overdue. We'd almost finished when the comp-board chimed.

I flipped on the big screen. Mon Balik appeared just the way I'd seen him on Illana five weeks or so ago.

Hard thin face, large cold eyes. "Good health to you, Trader."

"No thanks to you, Mon Balik," I replied.

He ignored my remark. "You owe us twenty thousand credits."

Ten for yesterday, ten for today. "Yes. Plus parking fee. Don't forget that."

"True." He smiled briefly. "When do you intend to deliver us the gold?"

"When you deliver my brother, Mon Balik. Alive."

"Really, Corbett, we're not barbarians."

"You could've fooled me."

Balik ignored me again. "Unfortunately we can't deliver your brother. He's being held on very serious charges."

"Such as?"

"Smuggling, attempted murder." Balik's smile tightened as though he relished what he was saying.

I wanted to reach out and shake that smile off his face. "But you'll notice, Mon Balik, he's been accused of nothing serious."

"I fail to see your humor, trader."

"No humor intended, Mon Balik. I mean that the Federation has a statement from Professor Silvernight on a certain attempted pirating in open space. That, Mon Balik, is a Federation offense, and *that* is serious, or didn't you know?"

"Silvernight is a doddering old fool. You can't believe what he says!"

"Tell that to the Federation, Balik. Now then, if you'll bring my brother with you when you come tomorrow to sign the delivery paper, we'll transfer at that time. I'll even provide the tape the Federation thinks it's going to use for evidence."

Mike, out of range of the screen's staring eye,

straightened as though I'd jabbed him. Balik also paused, staring at me. Obviously stalling, he shook his head. "Tomorrow is too soon."

"Not for me, Mon Balik."

"I'll let you know."

The screen went blank. I turned back to the table.

Mike burred. "What do you mean, you'll provide the tape. What tape?"

"The tape you made of my conversation with Silvernight this afternoon."

Halfhearted denial appeared in Mike's eyes, but then he laughed. "You can't have it, Gil. That's evidence."

Damn the Federation mentality! I slammed the chair against the table. "The hell with your evidence, Mike. If it gets us Ken back, they can have it. And a dozen more like it for all I care."

"Over my dead body!"

"Don't tempt me, Pelonyi!"

Beth gave us her marquessa look. "Stop it! You sound like children. Maybe there's a way—"

Beth was right, of course. By the time we'd finished the meal I thought I'd come up with a more acceptable plan. "Okay, Mike, let's make a duplicate. We'll give the original to Balik and you'll still have your evidence to hang Silvernight when you get back to Illana."

"Give Balik the copy—"

What did it matter? I shrugged. When the comboard chimed a few minutes later, I let Mike reach for it. And as soon as I heard Balik say they'd be here at Morning Four for the gold, I went back to bed.

Mike shook me awake at 00:30. "Gil, Doc Keeton is on board. Wants to look at your leg before they leave."

The Federation doctor was young, quick and efficient. He stripped the old plastiskin and applied new. "I told them not to let you up until today. What happened?"

"I don't hear too well."

"You won't walk too well if you don't give it more rest." He reached into his case. "Mike said you needed some daycaps. Here." He dumped a little package on the bed. "Courtesy of the house."

I grinned. "Who said the Federation never gives you anything?"

Standing, he shook my hand. "Take it easy, now. See you on Sandy in four days and we'll change that plastiskin again."

Feeling suddenly grim, I stared at him. "Who said we'd be on Sandy in four days?"

"Mike said—"

"Mike doesn't know what he's talking about."

"Well—" the doctor eyed me with uncertainty, "wherever you are, change it. I'll leave some plastiskin—it's important! I hate to see good work go down the drain." Digging in his duffel he pulled out a big tube of the dressing and tossed it on the bed next to the Daylon capsules. "Don't forget."

"Sure." He left, unreassured, and I rolled off the bed to dress. Outside the door I heard him say, "You ready to go?"

Beth answered. "Yes."

A hollowness invaded the pit of my stomach. I didn't want her to leave. But I couldn't very well ask her to stay, could I? No, let her leave. That's what she wanted. All the way along she'd gotten exactly what she wanted. I guess that's what happens when you're a marquessa's daughter. Whatever you want, you get. Even married to a trader, for a little while.

She appeared in the doorway. "Gil, I just wanted to say goodbye."

"Goodbye."

"Will you stop at Sandy on your way back?"

Not if I could help it. "Maybe. Don't know yet."

"Well, if you do, can I hitch a ride to Illana?"

I knew she didn't mean it. I smiled as much of a smile as I could muster. "Sure, why not?"

She reached up and kissed me on the cheek. The same one she'd slapped a little over a week ago. "See you on Sandy."

"Sure," I repeated.

When Mike came to the door a few moments later I was still standing where she'd left me.

"Where's Beth?"

As if he didn't know. "Gone." I pulled the shirt over my head.

"You really are one dumb bastard. I mean, to let something like that get away!"

I looked around for my boots and found them under the sleepboard.

Ignoring my lack of response, Mike continued. "Why didn't you ask her to stay?"

Sitting on the edge of the bed, I pulled the boot on carefully over the plastiskin. Deliberately put my mind to something besides what he was saying. The LEM. Had they brought it aboard? I stood into my other boot and started poking through the cupboards.

"And what's more you're not talking about it, is that it? What ae you looking for?"

"The LEM I had when you picked us up."

"I threw it in a drawer in the lounge."

He stood aside to let me pass. Tried again. "I mean it, Gil. You shouldn't have let her go."

"Pelonyi," I said, "shut up."

Only an hour later Balik signalled he was ready to come aboard. He was early by almost three.

154

"With Trader Corbett?" I asked.

Balik hesitated, but then agreed and the screen went blank.

"Balik's up to something." I could feel it in the marrow of my bones.

Mike nodded. For a brief moment we shared an uneasy anticipation. Then the Cargo One light flashed from red to green, indicating a docked shuttle. I released the door seal. "Let's go."

But Mike was already ahead of me, disappearing into the passageway.

Balik came aboard first. Cautiously. As though not sure what to expect. He glanced from me to Mike's dark face and back again. Smiled like a sand lizard. "I've come to take delivery of my gold."

"You know the terms."

He nodded, snapped his fingers and Ken stumbled into view. A guard was right behind Ken with a LEM. When Ken stopped, the guard put the LEM to the back of his neck.

Ken's face was haggard, there was no voluntary movement to his body. His clothes hung on him as though he'd not eaten in some time and his eyes were dull, but when he looked at me there was a spark—just a spark—of recognition. And something else. But the something else was gone before I could read it.

The recognition was enough. Relief flowed over me. I turned back to Balik.

"The gold," Balik said.

"The delivery receipt first," I said.

Coldly Balik smiled. "No, no delivery receipt, trader. Only the life of your brother."

I stared at him. The money in trust on Illana would revert to them if I didn't produce the receipt. He knew that as well as I did. Then I looked at Ken again. Drugged, probably DTC. Injured, who knew how

155

badly . . .

A savage anger rose in me. "No," I shook my head. "You've taken my ship and you've taken my brother—and ruined both." I laughed, and even to my own ears it had a crazy sound. "I've nothing else to lose by keeping your gold, Balik."

"Gil—" Mike began.

"Stay out of this, Pelonyi!" I snapped. The LEM I snatched from my belt felt good and solid in my hands. I pointed it at Balik. "In fact, Mon Balik, I've nothing left to lose by killing you."

Balik's jaw dropped. He turned to Mike. "You are a representative of the Federation. You cannot stand by and let this madman—"

I glanced at Mike. What would he do?

Mike hesitated, looked at me, and then at Ken. Leaned back against the wall and folded his arms. Shrugged. "Give him his receipt, Mon Balik."

I moved the Gabby away from the Ball Ten parking sphere at a little after Morning Four. The Eagle, with Beth and Silvernight aboard, had been gone for an hour and Balik and the Brothers contingent he'd brought to remove the gold had just left.

Mike now watched me from the flight recliner Beth had occupied the week before. Neither of us spoke of the session we'd just suffered through with Balik, and I thought we probably never would. Ken had collapsed on the sleepboard in the small sleeper.

Mike's jaw worked, but his voice was mild. "You handle this damned Class Four like it was a shuttle-bug."

I knew what was wrong. He was still angry, doubtless because I'd gone ahead and given the tape to Balik. But I'd given my word. And we did have Ken.

"So? No one invited you along, Pelonyi. You

156

could've stayed with the Eagle."

System Control came on with a caution to continue on minimum power until we were beyond the 20 KK surface limit. I said my favorite dirty word and kicked in pods three and six. The sooner we were away from this dark corner of the Cluster the better I'd feel. And I couldn't care less about disturbing their atmosphere. In their dark little holes, they probably wouldn't even notice.

The first hour was busy, but the Gabby's one-man control system put every control within reach—of an able bodied man which I found I wasn't yet.

Mike offered help, but I refused until we reached third orbit, the erratic orbit of the dead planet Ignatius. By that time I had to have a breather.

"Mike, check the star-comp and see if we've picked up a tail."

"Why? Do you expect one?"

"Don't you?"

He grunted an answer that could've meant anything and stepped to the star-comp. When he removed the cover I dimmed the lights so he could read the board easier. This close to Brother Timothy we'd pick up a busy field.

Finally he laughed. "There they are. How'd you know?"

"Easy. Remember the conversation with Silvernight?"

"Yes. He was pretty mad when he found your pods were normal Class Four!" The glow from the star-comp cast a ghoulish light up into his face. "You son of a—that's why you insisted on giving them the— you wanted them to come after us!"

Grinning, I shoved the Gabby's manual into comp-control and in-keyed a course to take us out of the system. Exactly. Ken was back but they still had the

Arabella, and I damned well wasn't letting them keep her if I could help it!

"Let's go see how Ken's doing."

13

Ken was doing badly. Mike had already given him a counteractant to the DTC, but more than DTC was wrong with him. Mike cursed the fact that the Federation doctor had left before Ken came aboard but knew better than to urge me on to Sandyminder.

Now we gave Ken a more thorough examination.

"Broken ribs, I think," Mike said. Gently he explored the bruises on Ken's stomach and side. "Could be some internal injuries."

"And a nasty cut on his head—" Part of Ken's dark head was matted with blood. I washed what I could. "And Balik said they weren't barbarians!"

"Bastards," muttered Ken. I grinned. That sounded like the brother I knew. He drifted off again.

Mike stood. "Why don't you get some rest too, Gil. It'll take us a good thirty hours to get out of the system. I can keep an eye on the comp and controls for a while."

I hesitated. Not that I thought him incompetent, but how much would he notice? But, what could he do now about anything he found? "All right. Let me check the core and fuel and then I'll take you up on that."

"Do you need any help?"

"No."

The white-suit still felt damp from the last time I'd used it, and the plastiskin around my left leg made it a tighter than usual fit. By the time I was suited I was tired, or maybe I'd been tired all my life.

Letting myself into Cargo Three, I locked the door behind me. The eight silver drums sat like gods on silver thrones. Each drum, taller than I, was strapped to the floor.

Unstrapping the first, I rolled it back toward the core hatch. Carefully. Treat them gently, Dunn had said. But the drum was only heavy until it reached the core room, and then it became merely awkward in the zero-G field.

What would Silvernight say if he could see me now? The thought made me grin again. And the nice thing was that, if I were careful, there was even enough to get the 'Bella back home.

So let them follow. They'd only get as close as I let them.

With only the blue glow of the core to work by, I packed the four auxiliary pods the way Dunn had shown me, white end toward the injectors and red end facing the core. When I put the empty drum back in place, Cargo three looked exactly the same as before.

Mike sat at the controls when I finally got through the de-con fog and unsuited again. I paused at the star-comp to assess our position. Still safe, but still being followed.

"Gil, it's been years since I pushed a Class Four. I don't remember this whole panel." Mike pointed at the new circuit control Dunn had installed for the aux-iliary pods. The one Federation had tried to stop us from ordering.

I looked over his shoulder pretending surprise. "Oh, that. Just an update. The Dunlevy Company does it every couple of years. Drops old circuits and

160

adds new ones." I wondered if he believed me.

I also checked the course on the star-comp. Not that I didn't trust him, but I didn't.

"Gil, where's this ship headed?"

"Back to Illana."

"Don't try to bull me, Gil. We're not heading toward an inward passage and we're not going to Sandy."

"I never said we were."

"Then where—"

A new note of urgency had entered Mike's voice. Something he was trying to hide. And questions hit me that I should've thought of before. Why had he really come with me? Where did he think we were going?

Suddenly I remembered his reaction when Silvernight mentioned KKS speed. A cold chill ran through me.

DTC my foot! KKS was more like it!

But why should I have expected anything different? It wasn't like we were still friends. But would he tell me . . .

"Mike, level with me."

He spun the First Control to face me, his eyes wary. "What do you mean?"

"I mean, what are you doing here? What's your real assignment?"

Cautiously he laughed. "You're beat, Gil. Why don't you follow your brother's example and get some sleep?"

I still had the LEM in my belt. Pulling it out, I pointed it at him. It wavered and I used both hands to steady it. "Mike, I'm not kidding. Tell me!" I sighted down the barrel. "Tell me or I'll blast you out of Control!" I meant each word.

"Gil—!" Mike choked. "Gil, don't be stupid!"

"I asked a question, goddammit, and I want an answer!"

"Dunlevy's pods!" Mike slid out of First Control and faced me, his hands spread out. Taking a step toward me he extended one hand.

"Stay right there, Mike. What do you know about Dunn's pods?"

"Only that they're experimental. That the Federation agreed to give Dunlevy, and consequently you, full protection in return for a chance to be the first in line when the pods are put on the market."

He spoke fast but, damn it, he lied! Dunn would never agree to that without telling me! "And the DTC charge?"

"It was the only thing I could think of to get me on board."

Another lie. If Beth's plan had worked, the charge would've been true. "You could have just told me—"

"And had you tell me to go to hell?" He took another step toward me. "Give me the LEM, Gil."

He was right. I'd have told him to go to—

He took another step. "Give it to me."

I tossed him the LEM. "Go to hell, Pelonyi."

"Go to bed, Gil." His voice shook. "I'll wake you when we hit the boundary."

I awoke in the semidarkness of the main sleeper thinking of the warm sands of Illana and of running down to the water's edge with Beth. But thinking of her hurt, so I thought of Pete instead. How was he? When would we hear? God, if I'd only told him about Dunn's pods, warned him to be careful—but Pete's greatest fault was that he could never keep his mouth shut. For years we hadn't told him anything but what we wanted all Illana to know. Well, Pete, I thought, good luck to you.

With a cautious movement I turned on the bed and the dull ache in my leg became a sharp, deep bite. "Oh hell!" I reached for the daylon.

A few moments later, when I crossed the passage to the other sleeper, I saw Mike at the star-comp staring down into its depths. He looked up and frowned. "You're supposed to be asleep."

Still angry with him, without answering I entered the smaller sleeper. Ken lay the way we'd left him, but his breathing was more regular and he had better color in his face. For a moment memories crowded in, memories of when we were kids—God, how I'd wanted to be like him! I'd wanted to walk like him, talk like him, I'd wanted the same girls he had. I'd wanted to be a partner in CTV the way he was. But after Dad died I'd been shut out of Ken's life completely and totally. Shunted off to the Federation Academy where I'd hated every minute of the regulation, the discipline. I hadn't understood it then and I still didn't understand it but suddenly it didn't matter any more. He was my brother and I'd finally done something for him he couldn't do for himself.

That was some small satisfaction.

Quietly I backed out and shut the door.

Feeling a hundredweight lighter I moved to Mike's side and looked down into the star-field. Mike pointed at the double light speck. "Right there. They've kept that distance for six hours now."

I went around and studied it from another angle then punched a request for readout. One hundred ninety kilometers distant. Our speed was 800 Ks and still climbing. Our lapsed time since reset was eleven hours and twenty-eight minutes.

Had I been asleep that long? "Did I reset when we left Timothy?" I couldn't remember.

"Nope. I did it when you checked the core."

I nodded, then smiled, thinking of the little scene I'd staged. Was Mike still upset? He didn't seem to be. I went back the galley for something to eat.

Later, fed and cleaned up, I felt almost human. I took Second Control and leaned back, liking the feel of the ship around me.

Mike watched me a short while, barely containing a frown. "You," he said finally, "amaze me. Thought you'd be out another five hours at least. Feel better?"

"Much." So much that I couldn't even stay angry with him. "Have you had any sleep?"

"I'm not tired."

Oh, no? Then why the sag to his shoulders, the dark circles around his eyes? Sure he wasn't tired. But that was his business. I let my fingers play lightly across the controls. Making sure he hadn't messed with any of the settings and another thought occurred to me. "Did you ever reach the Eagle?"

He darted a quick glance at me, then dropped his attention to his hands. "How did you know I tried?"

"How stupid do you think I am, Mike? The minute you found out we weren't following her to Sandy you tried to reach her." Although I was guessing, it was a damned good guess. I knew Mike. Nothing if not loyal—to Federation.

"I couldn't reach her."

"What'd you want to tell her?"

"Only our course change. So they wouldn't worry when we didn't show."

Or so she could follow us? "Where's she going after Sandy?"

"Back to Illana."

An uneasiness crept into my sense of well-being. Could I believe him? Was he telling the truth? God, I wanted to. I didn't want the Eagle in our way later on! But that thought brought up another. What would

Mike do when he discovered what I really had in mind?

Meet that problem when you come to it, Corbett!

The star-comp alarm went off. Mike hunched over the board and punched the readout. "Our friends are closing."

"How close?"

"Lying 160 now."

"What's the max effective range on an E-LEM?"

"Cannon that size—eight kilometers. You think they have one?"

I told Mike about Patterson Reed, the weapons expert who'd been resident at the school. A grim expression filled his face. He went back to the comp.

Then, after a short period of uneasy quiet he tightened. "Gil, they're closing again."

"Good." I flipped a switch that tied in the star-comp with the speedic and set it for a very gradual closure, silently thanking Dunn once more for his marvelous attention to these small details. Then I glanced around. When things are going smoothly I tend to get sloppy with my housekeeping. I picked up several cups and carried them back to the recycler and touched the button.

A hard thud came from the small sleeper next door. Ken's voice, clear and brittle. "Son of a bitch!" I started in, then thought better of it. If he awoke angry, no sense in making him more so. Shortly he appeared in the doorway, holding his side. We stared at each other. Then, unexpectedly, his face filled with relief. "Kid—am I ever glad to see you!"

I shrugged. "Even a stardrifter has his uses."

He grinned and turned—and saw Mike. His relief fled. "Who's Boy Wonder?" To Ken anyone in a Federation garb is a boy wonder.

"Mike Pelonyi, Ken. You remember—"

165

Ken spun on me, his face flashing quick pain. "Pelonyi, huh? I've heard of him." Then, ignoring Mike completely, Ken limped to the star-comp. "Where the hell are we?"

I felt the old angers stirring. "What do you care? As long as you aren't where you were?"

"Yeah, I guess . . ." Ken's voice trailed off. Leaning against the table he stared down into the board.

I saw Mike tense. He wasn't used to being ignored. But, hell with him. He was the uninvited guest. He'd be double uninvited when I told Ken how the FIS had dragged its heels this past eight months.

Keeping an eye on the two of them, I moved through the lounge on my clean-up tour, shelving loose tapes, pulling the rack down over the charts. If we lost the grav-pack I didn't want to dodge a ship adrift with unattached odds and ends.

"The way those fellows are closing they must be burning their cores," Mike said finally.

I joined them at the board. "Probably." When I touched Ken's shoulder he flinched and I hated to ask my next question. But I had to know. "Ken, think you can handle the Gabby?"

I felt a stillness in him. Met the question in his eyes. "I don't know kid. I can't load pods but I could probably handle controls. Why?"

Mike echoed the question. "Why? What are you going to do?"

I hesitated, but with the ships closing I couldn't put off telling them any longer. "I'm going to show you," I grinned, "how to steal a ship." I didn't give either of them a chance to argue with me. "Now Ken, if you'll get over to First Control and move her up to 1500, Mike and I'll go load pods."

Ken didn't argue. "What's on our tail?"

"Probably a Class Five and the 'Bella."

Ken dropped into the First Control seat. With bitterness heavy in his voice he wouldn't look at me. "Don't you mean the Monk's Retreat?"

"I mean the Arabella," I said quietly. "They only think they have a ship named Monk's Retreat. We know better."

Weakly Ken smiled. "They think—" Then his amusement vanished. "You haven't asked me what happened yet. Aren't you curious?"

"Silvernight told us."

"Silvernight?" Startled, Ken looked around. "Where'd you run into him?"

"He came aboard here. Before we left Timothy. He's on his way back to Illana on the Federation ship Eagle—"

"The hell he is!"

I chilled.

Ken continued, "He was on that damned shuttle that brought me from Timothy out to the Gabby!"

Mike burst out, "That's impossible!"

Raw antagonism sprang to Ken's battered face. "You calling me a liar?"

"No," I broke in quickly, "Mike's not calling you a liar. It even makes kind of weird sense. Silvernight knew he was facing charges if he went back to Illana —" I glanced at Mike for confirmation and Mike nodded "—and he probably figured he stood a better chance with Garrison."

Ken frowned. "From what I heard, they're paying him a small fortune to develop a high-speed fuel. And he had a pretty good one but it's not stable. Burnt out cores on two Class Fives when they tried to catch me." Ken gave me a weak grin. "Some chase, by the way."

Visualizing the surprise they must've felt when that defenseless Class Four walked away from them, I laughed. "I'll bet." But my amusement was short-lived. "Ken, this fuel of Silvernight's. Do you think that's what they're using in the 'Bella right now?"

"Probably."

"Would it make her faster than that Class Five?"

"Sure, but it'll damage her pods. Might even blow her core if they keep maximum thrust for any great time."

"How much revision would it require?" Enough to keep us from using Dunn's fuel?

Ken rubbed his stubbly chin. His anger was gone now, but his face was an unhealthy grey. How long could he stay on end? "They'd have to put additional shielding between the pods and the core. If Silvernight learned anything from that time he chased me he'd also find another way of cooling—" Ken's eyes narrowed. "Kid, what are you thinking?"

I smiled and shook my head. "Not sure, yet." Which only meant that I didn't want to say it yet.

But the revisions on the 'Bella were important. They didn't sound like they'd bar us from using her. Actually the only problem would be if they changed the shape of her fuel pods so that Dunn's fuel rods wouldn't fit.

Mike eyed me sardonically. "You know, Gil, there isn't much you can really do with your leg—"

Ken twisted around and looked and for the first time noticed the plastiskin. "What happened to you?"

I didn't want to go into it. "It's a long story. I'll tell you some day." Maybe the same day I'd tell him how close I'd brought the CTV to ruin!

The star-comp's alarm interrupted again and thankfully I turned back to the table. "Put it on the screen, Ken, and let's see what we have."

The big overhead screen lit up.

With disgust Mike stared down into the board.

"Look at them spreading out for the kill!"

"Ken," I said, still watching the screen, "edge her up to 1900 Ks then accelerate just enough to stay out of E-LEM range. We don't want any accidents."

Ken shot me a wry glance. "Aye-aye, *Captain*."

For a long moment my anger colored everything red. Ken always had had the ability to remind me that he was older, wiser—the guy in charge. Grimly I faced him. We might as well get it settled right now who was in charge here. "Ken—"

But he beat me to it. "Kid, it's your show. I never thought I'd see the day when I'd let you take over. But then, I didn't think I'd see many more days, period. I—" He looked away, swallowing, and the words came with effort. "I was never—so goddamned happy to see anyone in my life as I was to see you—makes a man think—" He cleared his throat and nodded at the screen. "That Class Five won't be able to keep up with us at 1900 Ks."

Tension flowed out of me. Later he might want to retract his words, but for the time being we were back in business. "That's what I'm hoping. What's the core-gauge say?"

"High normal, edging up. We've got 1600 Ks to go there."

"Okay, hold her steady." I turned to Mike, surprising a look of intense interest on his face. "You wanted to do something, so suit up and help me with the pods."

Mike nodded and started toward the passageway. I followed, but reaching the galley I turned and looked back at Ken. He was intent on the big screen. A strange feeling grew in me. Ken had changed these last nine months and so had I, but had we changed enough?

Dunn's pods looked so ordinary I could feel Mike's surprise even though I couldn't see his face through the visiplate of the white-suit.

"Hey, Gil, is this stuff for real?" His voice sounded high and far away. I nodded.

The fuel drums hadn't become any lighter. I showed him how to release one and roll it through the small hatch at the rear of Cargo Three. I also should've shown him how to handle it in the weightlessness of the core room, but I thought he knew.

The blue glow of the core filled every corner of the long room. The pods that I'd loaded earlier were in the first position and being used with a mixture of the normal fuel. That normal fuel was almost gone. To increase speed at almost twice the usual rate, which we were now doing, Ken would have to kick in the auxiliary pods.

We had to hurry. I went first, explaining how the rods went in. Mike nodded and I left him to it and went back for another drum of fuel for the other auxiliary.

Minutes later, just as I was shoving the last rod into place in the second set of pods, I heared Mike's anguished voice. "God, Gil, look out!"

I turned awkwardly. The fuel drum came tumbling down at me.

And beyond me the core . . . .

Only one thought entered my mind. If it hit the core we were dead. If it hit—

I grabbed the drum I'd just emptied. Shoved it with every ounce of strength I could toward the oncoming drum.

"Gil, jump!" Mike sounded desperate.

Better me than the core casing! I felt I was moving in molasses. For an eternity I travelled the three meters behind the drum I'd shoved.

Then the drums collided and one bounced high up. I grabbed out, and for a second felt the cloth of my white-suit catch. A new and wrenching fear turned my stomach.

Did it tear? Did my suit tear?

I twisted to watch the drum. It spun off, glanced off an auxiliary pod, then fell against the ball of the core and bounced away. I caught up with it and brought it under control.

Mike reached me. "Are you all right?"

I turned on him. "How did that drum get away?"

"Gil, I don't how. I just don't know."

"With friends like you, Pelonyi, I don't need enemies."

"Good God, do you think I did it on purpose?"

I pushed the drum ahead of me through the hatch to Cargo Three and let him get the other. He threw his in and I strapped them down. My silence made him ask again. "Well, do you?"

I pointed him to the decontamination shower. The panicky fear was still with me. Had the suit torn? I couldn't be nice about it.

Sitting in Second Control a short time later I went over the left sleeve of the suit with an airgun and enlarger lense, still worried that it'd been damaged. How could Mike have been so careless?

Beside me in First Control, Ken had charge of this ship. Our speed out of the quadrant was a steady 1950 Ks. Mike had fallen onto a lounge recliner and had been asleep in two breaths. Ken, his attention on the panels, asked, "Did you feel the difference when we kicked in Dunn's rods?"

I nodded.

Mike, on the recliner, snored softly. I glanced at him. He'd gone out as if he'd had a shot of DTC. How long since he'd had any sleep? Was it lack of rest that had caused the accident? Or something more complicated?

I didn't know. And not knowing scared me almost as much as the thought of a torn white-suit.

I went back to my examination and turned the suit slightly. There it was, at the cuff where it met the glove. The coating was scraped away. My stomach turned over again.

"Kid," Ken said suddenly, "what happened in there?"

"Nothing." I used the little air pressure nozzle, tried to force air from the inside through the small abrasion. It wouldn't go through the inner rubber coating. My heart stopped beating so hard. Applying liquid patch on the outside, I then held the suit on my lap for the few moments it took to dry.

Ken stared at me. "Nothing, huh? That's not what it sounded like on the monitor."

"I didn't know you were listening." I folded the suit for stowing and reached for a daycap. The extra activity had made my leg remember its pain.

Ken glanced at Mike. "I wouldn't trust a Federation man as far as I could throw him."

"You don't have to." I stood and my leg throbbed. "Mike's not your problem."

"No? What's he doing here?" A touch of the old criticism was back in Ken's voice. I felt a responding anger. This was the way all our fights started. His criticism, my defense. But it didn't have to be that way, did it? I took a deep breath. "Forget it, Ken. He's here and that's that."

Ken opened his mouth but before he could object I repeated it for good measure. "Forget it." Grabbing the white-suit I started off down the lounge toward storage.

"Kid," Ken snapped at my back, "do you know

what you're doing?"

I turned and grinned at him. "Do you, Ken?"

At first he seemed taken back. Then he laughed. "Hell, if we knew I guess we wouldn't be here, would we?" I shrugged. He went on, eyeing my leg, "Between us we might make one good pilot."

He was so right I had no comeback.

I was on my way back from the storage area five minutes later when the com-board chimed.

"That's the 'Bella trying to contact us," Ken said. "Want to answer?"

At least he was asking. Suddenly I felt better. "Is that Class Five still hanging on?"

"She's dropping back."

"How far?"

"About fifty kilometers behind the 'Bella, now."

And the 'Bella? I checked. Ken was holding her at 100 kilometers. What could they want? For us to stand still while they boarded? I shook my head. "Don't answer. And watch that Class Five. I want to know where she is every second!" I moved past Mike's recliner and he opened his eyes. "What's happening?"

"Nothing. Go back to sleep."

"Ummmm." He shut his eyes again and relaxed into the cushions.

Half an hour later the com-board chimed again, and this time it didn't stop. "Son of a bitch," growled Ken, "they won't take no for an answer."

I added a few choice words of my own, but the chime continued. "Okay," I said finally, "put them on the big screen and let's see what they want."

It was Silvernight. I flipped on the screen receiver but not the return eye. No sense letting him see how bad off we were.

"I know you can hear me, Corbett. And I'm sure we can come to some agreement." He smiled and it was a diffident, ingratiating expression. How could anyone doubt him? I slammed off the receiver.

"Ken, what's maximum com-board range?" I thought I remembered something like five hundred Ks.

"Thousand to fifteen hundred Ks for our units. Why?"

"I was hoping we could move out of range of the com-board."

Ken grinned but shook his head. A moment later he said, "Approaching KK speed. And it looks as though we're losing that damned Class Five."

I moved to the star-comp table. Ken was right. The Brothers ship spun off in a wide arc. No doubt about it. She was heading for home. I punched a quick calculation into the star-comp memory and pulled down a chart for Quadrant One.

"Kid—" a new fear entered Ken's voice. "They're pushing the 'Bella to her limit. They'll burn her out trying to keep up!"

I nodded. Fitting the star chart for the quadrant over the comp table I checked our course. Our projected pathway was taking us to the far side of the Juno Colonies. And then—I smiled—nothing. We had reached the end of our cluster. And there was nothing else out there for fifty light years.

I watched a while longer, until there was no doubt the Five would indeed head for home. Then I nodded. "Okay, Ken. Cut the thrusters and hold her at 2Ks. We'll put her on comp-control and get some rest." I shoved the quadrant map back into its slot and set the star-comp to warn if the 'Bella came within the limit. I went back for coffee for both of us.

Ken rested where he sat at First Control with part of

his attention still on the starview and part watching the core gauges. I set his cup on the arm of First Control and dropped down next to him.

Ken nodded his thanks then turned the control so he could also take in Mike. Finally he said, "It wasn't a lot of talk. You really do have something in mind to get the 'Bella back, don't you?"

I grinned. "That's what it's all about. First you, and now the 'Bella."

"You're taking a big chance." His eyes grew darker. "Not that I don't appreciate it—"

I wondered if I'd ever get up nerve enough to tell him that it hadn't started out as this kind of plan. Probably not.

He stared at Mike. "Is he part of it?"

"Not a great part." I told Ken what Mike had said about protection for Dunn's pods and fuel. Ken snorted his disbelief.

Then the com-board chimed again and at the same moment Mike turned over. He hadn't been asleep. He'd been listening. A cold feeling washed over me followed by a sense of urgency. I spun back to the screen. "Put the call on."

Silvernight appeared again. "Your core is heating up, Corbett," he started as soon as he knew we were listening. "You won't run away from us. You can't."

"More of the same?" Mike sat up, stretched and rubbed at his eyes.

I leaned over to First Control. The core gauges read high normal. Holding steady. "He's only hoping."

Ken nodded. "He's basing it on the fact we cut our thrusters."

"If I can't convince you, Corbett," Silvernight chuckled, "maybe someone else can."

Ken laughed. "Bull. Let's shut him—"

Beth appeared on the screen.

14

The autocratic smile was still on Beth's face, but her eyes were angry. "Gil, I told him this wouldn't work. But he doesn't understand—"

Ken spun First Control to face me. "Who the hell is that?"

I couldn't answer. I felt paralyzed. Even my mind refused to function except on the most rudimentary level. Beth! How had she gotten there? Why was she doing this?

Mike came to his feet. "Beth?"

Then suddenly I was thinking again. "Mike, get over here. Take the view-com. Tell them Trader Corbett died from his wound two hours ago and they're wasting their breath!"

"But who is she?" Ken repeated.

"That," I said, the ache still there, "is my wife."

Mike grabbed my arm as I moved out of his way. "It's cruel to tell her that."

I shook him off. "Cruel? She'll be relieved." I moved out of the range of the viewer.

Ken watched me with ludicrous disbelief. "How many other things haven't you told me?"

"Shut up and listen."

Mike gave Beth the message in a way that indicated he hated every word he had to say. And she believed him. She stared at him and tears welled in her eyes. "Oh, Mike, I'm—I'm sorry."

Ken gave me a funny look.

Beth disappeared abruptly from the screen and Silvernight took her place. "It doesn't change anything. In fact it makes matters easier, I must say. The younger Corbett was too stubborn for his own good. And yours. Why, he would've gotten you ki—"

Mike slammed the com-board off and spun on me. "You satisfied now?"

I was stung to reply. "Mike, damn it, do you think I enjoyed it?"

"Yes. Yes I do!" He slid out of Second Control and pushed by, stomped down the length of the lounge and disappeared into the passageway.

I turned to find Ken livid with anger. "I should've known there'd be a girl mixed up in it somewhere!"

"Damn it, Ken!" But what good was it trying to explain? Anyway, there was no time. I took a deep, shaky breath. Forced myself to think ahead. "It's time to jettison those empty drums. And anything else that's not pinned down. Make it look like we're stripping to save fuel."

Ken's face tightened. "And then what?"

"Then I'm going out."

Ken's anger evaporated to an expression of worry. He eyed my leg. "Can you do it?"

"Won't know until I try."

Mike came back in time to hear my words. He looked grim but controlled. "Try what?"

"Boarding the 'Bella."

He shook his head. "You're crazy! In your condition you'd never make it." He turned away. "Anyway, how could you get inside? Doesn't a Class Four seal in flight like the bigger ships?"

"She's got an emergency door on the core section

177

for inflight repairs," Ken said, "but it's a keyed lock."

"And I know the key," I said. "And while I'm busy doing that you'll sit here and negotiate with Silvernight. Keep him occupied."

"The hell I will!" Mike's jaw jutted out with determination. "You can't take that ship by yourself! You don't even know how many people are on board her."

"I can face that problem when the time comes."

"We'll face it together, you mean."

I forced a grin. "Why Mike, and you a Federation! Stooping to piracy? What would Commander Sinclair say?" But then I thought about it and the seriousness of what he offered hit me. "You're the one's crazy." Abruptly I stopped. If he wanted to risk his position with the Federation Service Arm, why should I stop him? I didn't owe him a damned thing!

Over the next hour we jettisoned anything we could find, including the empty drums that had held Dunn's fuel. Finally it was time to suit up and go.

I had a last word with Ken. "If I'm not on that comboard in two hours to tell you everything's okay, you kick in Dunn's pods and head for home!"

Ken's face was a study in conflicting emotion but he didn't argue. He merely pointed out the obvious. "Two hours isn't much time."

Even in the insulated tightsuit with its bulky life support pack I was icy cold. I lost all sensation of up and down. I knew I was spinning because the universe spun around me but I didn't feel it as spin. I was the center of the universe. I lost the star that was the 'Bella and floated.

Behind me I glimpsed Mike using short bursts of the little hand propulsion unit to right himself. When I did the same the universe felt less like a spinning top.

And after I lined myself up on the Gabby's blue tail-glow, I once more found the moving light that was the 'Bella.

Floating, I had no sensation of speed. With no point of reference except distant Juno and the closer Brothers, we were only debris floating in absolute silence through cold.

Were we drifting too fast? Using the hand unit I came around to face Mike and held up my gloved hand to tell him to brake more. He nodded.

We floated for about twenty minutes, letting the 'Bella slowly approach. Her course was erratic but if I were her pilot, I'd also be worried about plowing through the debris.

At one kil she started to swerve away from us and Mike touched my arm. I shook my head. Let her go around. Each time they had to expend energy maneuvering, they had that much less for speed.

We were abreast of the 'Bella's Cargo Two door when I motioned to Mike that it was time to move.

After the cold of space, the heat of the core chamber suffocated me. Even through the suit I could feel the fire of the too-high rate of consumption of her fuel. Damn it, they'd ruin her! The core would go critical!

Didn't they know that? Didn't they care?

Passing through to the de-con chamber, I saw what Ken meant about increasing her shields. Big, heavy lead plates had been welded around the chamber walls increasing her weight by at least ten thousand bars. But the pods looked normal. My relief came in waves. They hadn't modified her to the point we couldn't use her!

Stepping from the de-con chamber to the storage passageway outside the cargo doors a few moments later, I came face to face with a Brothers security guard. Even though he had a LEM at his belt, he was too startled to think of it. I hit him and he doubled over with a soft groan. A rush of weakness flowed over me. Leaning against the storage wall, I caught my breath, then stripped off my visiplate. Mike, right behind me, was doing the same. He noted the man on the floor with approval. "Couldn't have done it better myself. Where shall we put him?"

"Tie him up and put him in Cargo Two."

Mike assented. We kicked off our suits and Mike scooped the guard off the floor. I looked for a place to stow our gear where it wouldn't be noticed.

Mike was right. It would be handy to know how many people were on board. Silvernight, Beth and at least one guard, but who else? A pilot, of course. Four. I opened a storage cabinet. Unfamiliar gear filled the shelves. I shoved the tight suits in on top and then followed Mike on to Cargo Two.

The middle cargo room was full, mostly with furnishings and panelling torn from the lounge, repair gear from the lockers down the passageway, and extra lounge recliners and sleepboards. Everything was shoved in with no mind paid to order. God, what had they left behind?

Mike turned the guard on his stomach and used his own belt to bind him. I pushed through the mess to the door to Cargo One. The little viewplate was fogged and I wiped it with my sleeve. "An E-LEM, Mike. Look at that!" The big machine was right next door, cradled in a retractable pod.

"You sure that's what it is?"

I nodded. The crystal shape of the matrix was unmistakable.

Mike came over for a look and whistled softly. "Well, you figured that. Had she gotten close enough, she could have blown the Gabby right out of existence!"

"Or any other ship she didn't like, including Federation!"

"Damned right!" He rubbed the glass, trying to clear it. "How are they getting access to the outside?"

"Through the cargo port."

"That means they'd have to bring her around broadside. Can we get in there to dismantle it?"

I studied the door, noted the seal, and pointed it out to Mike. "Not without a tightsuit." But did we have to dismantle it? Did we have enough time? I touched my hour badge. No.

"One of us has to suit up again—" Mike began.

"No, we won't. We'll get through to Silvernight first." I turned back and headed for the passageway.

Mike grabbed my arm. "Gil, I've been watching you. There's no way you can take on that room full of guards and Silvernight and God knows who else."

"So who's going to do it? You? Mike Pelonyi versus the bad guys? Don't make me laugh, Mike. Come on, we're wasting time."

"Gil, damn it, listen to reason." A curious intensity entered his voice. "This is my job. It's what I'm paid for."

All my earlier doubts came flooding back. I stared at him, tried to read beyond the tight lips and intense eyes. What did he have in mind? "All right," I said finally, "we'll do it your way."

Mike grinned his relief. "I'll help you suit up again."

I pushed him toward the door. "No, we don't have time. You go on, see what you can do about Silvernight. I'll take care of this thing."

I watched Mike move down the long, shadowy passageway toward the galley, a big, broad-shaped figure in the dim light, and all my doubts came flooding back. All my formless suspicion. I damned well

181

wouldn't put on that tightsuit. No way. When Mike slipped into the L-shaped turn and disappeared, I silently followed.

Pausing in the L a moment later, I crouched; the voices were only a murmur coming from the lounge. How many? I strained to hear.

The first thing clear was Beth's sharp, "No, I don't understand. This is a criminal thing you are doing and I demand—"

I almost smiled. In this situation she could demand all she wanted, but it wouldn't get her anywhere with Silvernight.

Then another voice. Garrison! "Beth, dear, you have no choice. When we've converted Corbett's other Class Four, Minder will not be able to resist us."

"You won't get anywhere near Minder in either ship!"

"Not even when we tell the Marquessa we have you?" Garrison's voice chided gently.

"The Federation," said Mike, "would not approve."

Beth gasped and a shocked silence fell over the lounge. With a sigh of relief I started to straighten up, when Garrison spoke. "But what Federation doesn't know it can't disapprove, isn't that right, Mr. Pelonyi?" He laughed. A chilling sound. I caught my breath and froze. Garrison went on, "I didn't hear a docking alarm. Would you mind saying how you came aboard?"

"I came with Corbett. We did a space drift from the Gabby."

"You told us," said Silvernight acidly, "that he was dead."

"I said what he told me to say."

"And where is he now?" That was Garrison again.

"He's gone around to disengage your E-LEM."

"He must not touch it! He must not!" That was a new voice, vaguely familiar. Patterson Reed's?

"Let him get into the cargo room and you have him," Mike said. "You need him, in fact. In less than twenty minutes the Gabby'll walk away from you if he's not on that screen to tell his brother to bring her around."

The blood pounded in my ears. How could he? What did he hope to gain? He was betraying everything he'd ever believed in!

"Mike," Beth choked, "how could you? He's your friend!"

"Beth, dear," said Garrison, "don't be naive. No friendship is worth more than a million in gold credits!"

"Garrison," Beth's anger gave her clarity. "How can you be sure he isn't lying? He could be, you know. I'll bet Federation—"

Mike broke in with a laugh. "I've delivered. That's how he knows."

"That remains to be seen," Garrison said coolly.

"Oh, you're all despicable!" Beth shouted.

"Garrison," said Mike, "you'd better do something about her or she'll blow the whole deal. And, by the way, Corbett got one of your men. He's back in Cargo Two."

"Yes, of course." Garrison grunted a sharp command.

"Don't you dare touch—"

The sound of a smack made me cringe. Mike said softly, "Was that necessary?"

"Merely taking your idea to its logical conclusion. Get her out of here. How much time do we have, did you say?"

I lost the answer to that in the shuffle and grunt of someone lifting . . . Then I caught a glimpse of a black and red uniform approaching, and I faded back into the shadows of the storage area. Beth was a limp burden in the guard's arms and he went by without looking into the shadows where I crouched.

But he couldn't help seeing me on his way back.

In the dark I groped in a cupboard until I found a smooth metal object. It felt like the tripod leg for a con-light. It'd do.

Where was the guard taking Beth? Back toward the catch-all cargo area? He'd find and bring back the other guard! A sense of urgency pushing me on, I followed him. Quietly. Hardly daring to breathe.

Softly Beth groaned. She was coming around. The guard muttered under his breath. Stopping by the door, he set Beth on her feet. She swayed and he steadied her with one hand while he whirled the door lock with the other. Hearing my step he glanced backward.

I cracked the bar down on the side of his neck cutting off his incipient yell.

Beth's face drained of color. "Oh, Gil!"

"Hush!" I finished what the guard started with the door and pulled him through to rest beside the other guard. Beth followed and I motioned to her to shut the door.

It shut with a sigh and she turned and again tried to speak. "Mike—he—"

"I know. I heard." I took the LEM from the guard's belt and stuck it in my own. Had Mike taken the other? He must have, because it wasn't there. "Help me tie this guard."

Beth nodded. Her eyes were dark with anxiety and her hair tousled. Even her dark blousey tunic was wrinkled, but she was still the most beautiful girl I'd ever met.

And along with that thought came another. I still

loved her more than anything else in the whole wide universe!

I wanted to reach out to touch her and tell her so. But then I thought of the autocratic Marquessa of Sandyminder. She had raised her daughter for more than marriage to a mere stardrifter. But maybe, some day, I could lay claim to being something more than that.

Beth seemed to read me better than I read myself. All at once she was in my arms, her face buried against my shirt. "Gil," her voice was softly muffled, "I love you. No matter what happens, I do love you. And I'm so thankful it wasn't true—that you weren't—dead!"

I thought of all the things I wanted to say. And knew I'd never say them. Gently I kissed her hurt cheek. "Later," I smiled down at her. "Just remember you said it."

Her answering smile touched her eyes with a warmth reminiscent of the beach at Illana. "I won't deny it."

We secured the second guard and Beth surveyed our handiwork. "What next?"

I checked my hour badge. We still had eight minutes before Ken would take the Gabby home. "We have a LEM. If we had another we might try taking them." Mike included. "How many are on board?"

She frowned, thinking. "Seven—no, eight, counting Mike."

"Counting Mike," repeated a voice from the doorway. Mike, of course!

I turned, reaching for the LEM, but the one in his hand stopped me cold. Beth drew a sharp breath.

Mike held his LEM a little higher. "I know how to to use this too, remember?"

Anger rose in me like a high fever. I stared at Mike through a red haze. But the moment to move had passed. He motioned toward the passageway. "This way, kiddies. Let's go see teacher."

For a moment I couldn't understand. Then it hit me! He hadn't seen the LEM at my belt! Putting an arm around Beth, I drew her close and the LEM jabbed her in the side. She started to pull away, but I held her tightly.

Mike gave us a crooked grin and backed off far enough so I couldn't jump him as we went by. "You'll notice, Gil, I have great respect for your persistence, if not your intelligence."

We came to a stop facing him. Beth had given up trying to pull away. Her hand behind my back was working the LEM out of my belt.

"What's that supposed to mean, Pelonyi?"

"That means if you try anything, I'll blast Beth."

Shocked outrage sprang to Beth's eyes and for a moment she was very still. But this wasn't the time or the place to try Mike. He was too ready for it.

I settled for words. "You don't have the guts, Pelonyi."

"Don't I? Try me."

The sound was right. The hardness in his voice. I had no choice but to believe him.

Preceding him down the dark passageway and through the small galley, we emerged together into the stripped-down lounge. In the brighter light I looked again at Beth. The LEM wasn't in evidence, but I was reassured to know it was there—somewhere.

When we entered, Silvernight lifted his head. No surprise touched his face. "I told you that was the only other place he could be."

Reed, in a straight metal chair at a long table looked up from a sheaf of papers. He seemed annoyed. "You again!" He went back to his papers.

Silvernight chuckled that benign little laugh that

went so poorly with what I now knew about him. "Reed has no patience with meddlers. Garrison, sit him in that control. He must contact his ship."

"There's no way you'll make me do that," I said.

"You don't have a choice," said Garrison. He reached out, grabbed Beth's arm and twisted. She choked back a cry and lifted her chin. Her mother would've been proud.

Garrison's mouth tightened and he pushed her away. "We're running out of time." He faced the pilot sitting in First Control. "Raise the Gabby."

I laughed. "That won't do any—"

"Shut up!" Garrison shoved me into the Second Control seat. He placed the LEM against my cheek. "Put him on the screen."

"You won't convince my brother of anything! He won't come around just because he sees this." He damned well better not, anyway!

"I think you underrate his loyalty to you."

Ken's loyalty? I wanted to laugh again. Ken's only loyalty was to the Corbett Trading Venture. And that, at the moment, was just the way I liked it!

Ken appeared on the screen. Momentary confusion filled his eyes. Then a brief I-told-you-so look.

Garrison smiled and that same prickly sensation that I'd had when I first saw him crawled down my arms. Garrison's hand tightened on the LEM. "Your brother, Captain Corbett, has five minutes to live unless you bring that ship around and let us board her."

Ken looked a question at me.

"Get the hell out of here—" I started.

The LEM cracked down on my face before I could duck. I blinked painful stars.

"Five minutes, Captain," Garrison warned.

Anger cracked in Ken's voice. "Go to hell, Garrison."

When I could see again the screen had gone blank and Garrison had moved away. Now he leaned over the star-comp and stared into its depths, his face tense.

I studied the others one by one. The mask of Silvernight's smile was frightening. His tongue darted over dry lips. He, too, stared into the star-comp, his hands grasping the edge of the table, his knuckles white. Patterson Reed still looked at the big blank overhead screen as though he expected it to jump to life. Mike was watching me, his face guarded. The only one who seemed unconcerned whether or not the Gabby turned was the pilot.

I looked at Mike again and knew how it felt to hate. I'd never hated anyone before in my entire life the way I hated him!

If I had had the LEM at that moment I'd have killed him and then been glad to suffer the consequences. I dropped my gaze to my hands. I hadn't realized they were shaking.

Beth came to my side. The marquessa look was still uppermost in her face, but her voice softened. "You're bleeding."

I felt my head, my hand came away sticky. "Just a cut. Nothing serious."

"Will your brother come around?"

"I hope not."

She half turned and I saw the LEM outlined under her blouse. With a movement that would've done credit to a magician she slipped it out and dropped it into the seat at my side and at the same time retrieved a piece of silky scarf from her pocket. With tender care she touched the scarf to the side of my head, mopping blood.

"Beth," Mike said, "get over here and sit down. You're in the way."

"Of what? Your line of fire?" Her smile was cold.

I moved a little to let the LEM slide deeper into Second Control's seat. Beth lifted her chin again, that old flag that said she wanted to argue but I caught her hand. "It's all right. Do as he says."

She handed me the silky scarf and stalked to the farthest recliner.

We waited and the tension built. Silvernight's breathing became harsh. Finally the pilot turned. "Garrison, we're heating. I have to cut the thrusters."

"Not yet!"

"Soon, damn it!"

"Not until I tell you!" Garrison shouted.

I became supersensitive to the high whine of the laboring core. Even with Silvernight's cooling system it was burning up! I reached out to bring down the bar myself. Garrison grabbed my arm.

Suddenly Silvernight turned from the star-comp, leaned over and stared at the core gauge. His face blanched. "19—cut her back! She'll blow!"

Garrison flushed. He spun on Silvernight. "You said we could do it! You said there wasn't a ship in existence that could outrun us! You said we—"

Silvernight seemed to turn deaf ears to Garrison's tirade. He snapped at me, "How much greater speed can the Gabby attain?"

"I have no idea," I said truthfully.

Patterson Reed turned from the blank screen. "Use the E-LEM!"

Silvernight shook his head. "The range is too great."

"You might cripple her enough to—"

"All right!" Tensely, Garrison stared into the star-comp. "Cut speed and bring her around." He stopped short, his anger becoming icy contempt. "Wait—wait. He's *slowing*."

No, damn it! NO! Ken couldn't! Not now! I saw a

glint of satisfaction flash on Mike's face and my hate became fiercer. If I only got one shot, just one, I knew who it would be at.

"Use the E-LEM anyway," Reed grumbled. "I want to see if it does much damage."

Beth stared at him. "You're mad!"

Reed didn't hear. Nodding, nodding, he rubbed his hands together. "At 80 Ks we should get a disability effect of sixty percent. At fifty we can blow a hole in her side. Providing of course that we don't miss her altogether."

Garrison winced. "Shut up, Reed!" Garrison sounded as though he'd had his fill of genius experts.

Silvernight still watched the core gauges. Pulling out a handkerchief he mopped his face. "Now," he said softly, "it has to be now!"

"But—" Garrison began.

Silvernight cut him off. "Drop it now or we'll all go up with her!"

"All right!" Garrison snapped.

The pilot's hand darted to the panel, he slammed down and the high, dangerous whine of the core slowly dropped to a more reasonable level.

I took time to breathe again.

"Just a point of curiosity," said Silvernight, "how do you keep the core from heating up?"

"I don't know," I answered truthfully.

Reed snorted. "You won't get any help from him! Use the E-LEM. Bring that ship to heel!"

Beth was right. The man was truly crazy! And because he was, he was more frightening than the others. They at least, were predictable!

"Contact Captain Corbett again," Garrison said. "Tell him to stop and let us board him."

Silvernight chuckled. "Stop? My good man, he can't stop. Not without throwing the retros—"

Garrison't fat chin trembled with angry frustration. His look alone should have withered Silvernight's hair. "You tell him to come around so we can board! Tell him, damn you!"

15

Silvernight punched the compboard.

Instantly Ken appeared.

Silvernight smiled. "Bring her around, young man, and let us dock. We'll use the connector."

Garrison stepped to my side, raised the LEM to my ear. "Or else!"

Ken glanced away. He managed a slight shrug. "Whatever you say." I wanted to yell at him but I knew it wouldn't do any good. He looked as though he'd taken all he could take.

With no warning Garrison grabbed my arm and hauled me out of the Second Control seat. Desperately I thought of the LEM, half fell, and used the control arm to pull myself up. When I regained my feet I'd also regained the LEM. It was hidden in my belt under my arm. I prayed they wouldn't notice.

Beth jumped to her feet. "Gil, are you all right?"

"Yes."

Garrison pushed me past the star-comp and I glanced into its depths as I went by. The Gabby and the 'Bella were two specks of fast-closing light.

Suddenly Mike's bulk cut off my view. "Let's put them in the smaller sleeper. It has a lock."

Garrison nodded and shoved me toward the open sleeper door. Beth followed and the door hissed shut behind us. We were left in darkness.

Beth moved close and started to speak but I shushed her. Through the closed door I could hear Mike softly speak. "You don't need any of them. I can pilot that Class Four for you."

The hell he could! I touched the LEM at my belt. Thought of the years I'd known him. Even if he could, I wouldn't give him the chance.

Beth touched my arm. "Gil, how long before the Gabby comes around?"

"Probably fifteen or twenty minutes. We've cut the thrusters and my guess is Silvernight's about out of fuel. Someone'll have to go back and reload pods. Ken has a lot left but he wouldn't waste it making any sudden stops. I guess Silvernight's fuel isn't so hot after all."

Beth nodded. "Garrison's furious with him." In the dark I felt her deep sigh. "Almost as furious as he was with me when he found out we were married."

I thought about that. About Garrison who must've felt he had the whole situation under contol. About the Baliks, Min and Mon, who were playing some other game, a much larger game, than space pirate. "Beth, what were you supposed to do? I mean, instead of marry me?"

"I was only supposed to make sure you came back with the gold and the—the DTC." Shame tinged her voice. "I'm—so—sorry—about that, Gil." She drew a deep breath and her voice steadied. "It seemed so important that we should have the gold for the school. Garrison said if we got you arrested it would be so easy. I believed him!" Her voice dropped to a soft whisper. "It was a horrible thing to do—I just didn't realize *how* horrible . . . . Can you forgive me?"

For an answer, I pulled her to me and kissed her. Finally she drew back. "What do we do now?"

I couldn't answer her. Suddenly more tired than I'd ever felt in my life, I sank down against the door. Beth came down beside me and leaned her head on my shoulder. Closing my eyes, I felt drained. Drained of emotion, drained of energy.

"Did you know it was Balik's men who tried to kill us by burning a hole in the Gabby's nose?"

Beth trembled in my arms and I held her tighter. "I didn't know they hated me that much."

It was only a guess, but I'd bet a true one. Balik must have been absolutely furious to see his plans go awry. I thought of something else. "How did you get here from the Federation ship?"

Autocratic indignation stiffened her. "Silvernight! I thought he was through with them. He'd seemed so—so relieved to get off Brother Timothy! And then a Brothers shuttle docked on some pretense or other. Someone wanted to talk to him. He begged me. Said he was afraid to face them alone. I believed him."

"Didn't the Federation fellows know you were gone?"

"Probably not until it was too late. They'd assigned me to a cabin and I was going to sleep for ten hours. I told them I didn't want to be disturbed."

I could even hear her saying it! And I knew just how those fellows felt!

"Gil, I heard Silvernight say the only reason he came away from the School was because he hoped to see what made your ship run."

I nodded again. That figured. I felt my hour badge. Time crept by.

The next minutes were the longest of my life. I could hear very little through the door. Mike must've been standing very close to let me hear his lie. But I could feel the retros firing and felt us slew sideways. I told Beth what was happening and she wanted to

194

know how I could tell. I tried to explain that when you spend the best part of your life on a ship like the 'Bella or Gabby you feel her even through the soles of your boots.

Then came a jar that even Beth felt. "What's that?"

"I think—wait!" I heard close voices again through the door and came to my feet straining with every nerve to hear what was said.

First Garrison. "I'll go aboard with Abbott. You stay here with Silvernight and Reed."

"I can't study the core from here!" Silvernight protested. "I can't test the fuel by long distance!"

Abbott? One of the guards? The third guard?

"All right, then, you senile old fool. Come with me. But stay out of the way! No telling what Corbett will do."

Someone chose that moment to bump against the door, and I heard the soft slide of the lock and felt that old, familiar prickle of fear.

Was it deliberate? Or accidental? Why would someone out there have opened the door? I stood there flooded by suspicion. What would happen if we tried to go through?

Well, damn it, only one way to find out. "Beth," I whispered, "whatever happens, stay clear of it. Do you understand?"

I felt her resistance, then heard her whispered assent. Carefully I eased the door open a fraction and put my eye to the crack. Mike stood, half turned away from me, staring down into the star-comp, his shoulders hunched, tense. The pilot concentrated on his controls. Reed paced, annoyance on his face, petulance in his muttered words. I caught snatches of "won't let my try it—don't know why not—safer than trying to board—show them—"

195

He looked straight at my tiny crack and smiled, then deliberately turned his back. He'd done it! No doubt about it. Crazy old man!

I waited until Reed moved by the door again, then slid it all the way back. Reed was an easy target. With only a small regret I smashed down on the back of his head with the LEM. Mike heard him fall, whirled and reached for his own weapon.

"You touch that," I yelled, "and I'll kill you!"

He froze. "Gil—how—don't do anything foolish!"

"I don't intend to." The pilot turned. His face paled. He was almost hidden by Mike's huge frame and I moved to one side to that I could watch both. "You, what's your name?"

"Sarcy."

"Sarcy, move this ship away from the Gabby."

"We can't. We have the connector out."

The connector! Of course. That was the jar we'd felt. I envisioned the flexible docking tube shaking out like an umbilical cord from the 'Bella's passageway— an easy path for Garrison and Silvernight to the Gabby! "Bring it in."

Mike's face tightened. "No, Gil. Don't stop them. Let them board. You might kill them both if you pull loose now."

"No loss."

"Gil, you have to let them board!"

"They aren't setting one foot on my ship!"

"Gil, damn it, if you stop them now you'll ruin everything!"

"Yes," I said, "that's exactly what I'm going to do. Ruin everything! All your pretty plans and extra million and the whole works! Sarcy, I said pull it in!"

Sarcy reached out for the connector control but Mike turned on him furiously. "Don't touch it!" He turned back to me, pleading. "Gil, listen! Until they've boarded your ship there's no Federation crime they can be charged with. You have to let them board!"

"Hell with Federation!" I aimed down the LEM's barrel at Sarcy's startled face. "Last time, Sarcy. Pull loose!"

Mike tapped the star-comp. "Gil, look in here and you'll see."

I tightened my hand on the trigger lever of the LEM.

Mike moved faster than I thought possible. A heavy rimmed star chart came flying through the air at me. Simultaneously I ducked and shot. A harsh, wounded groan came from someone. Who'd I hit? I had a sudden, fierce hope that it was Mike. Then he was on me, his weight like a hammer knocking the breath out of me. We went down together.

When he hauled me to my feet his face was an angry, hurting mask. "Nobody could ever tell you a damned thing!" He pushed me down the lounge toward the star-comp. "Look in there and tell me what you see, goddammit!"

I looked because I had no choice. I saw two Class Fours surrounded by four Class Six Federation ships!

Where they'd come from I had no idea. I couldn't think. Why hadn't the comp alarm gone off? Were they really Federation ships? How could they be anything else?

I glanced at Sarcy. The Brothers pilot had turned his control and watched us with indecision.

Mike said, as much to him as to me, "It'll all be over shortly."

Slowly the true nature of what I'd seen filtered into my numbed mind. Federation! "You've—used our ships—for a Federation setup?" I stared at him through a boiling angry haze. "You've used—" No!

No they wouldn't! Not with Corbett ships!

With a speed that seemed almost slow, as though time held its breath, I whirled around, slammed the disconnect before Sarcy could move, before Mike could stop me. A jar went through the ship.

Mike leaped forward, his face white. "You fool! You damned stubborn fool!"

Mike was almost on me and I could see the pain in his face. The frustration. I wanted to reach the com-board. Tell Ken to run! *"To hell with the Federation!"* I shouted. Fireworks exploded in my head.

The next thing I knew I was on the gravity grid with Beth bending over me. I felt my jaw. It hurt like hell! The pilot Sarcy was nowhere in sight but Mike stood at the com-board. "Yes sir, that's what I said. They're trapped in the connector. If one of them should panic—"

Another voice, older, calm, said, "See what you can do from your end. How badly are you hurt?"

"It's not killing me."

Too bad, I thought. I struggled to sit up. I had to see the star-comp. What was Ken doing? The minute he saw Federation ships he should've pulled away. But did he?

Mike glanced at me. "About Corbett, sir—"

"Take care of Garrison and Silvernight first. Then we'll discuss it."

"Yes sir." Mike slammed the com-board off. Hurried by me toward the passageway. "You and your damned Federation phobia. A year's work down the drain."

"Go to hell!" I muttered at his back. He disappeared into the dark beyond the galley passageway.

"What is he talking about, a year's work?" Beth asked.

"How should I know?" But I had a good idea. I

pulled myself up to the star-comp table. Stared down at the grouping. My guess was right. A Federation setup. With the Federation using Dunn's pods and our ships as bait for the pirates! But why?

Why us?

Because of our reputations as anti-Federation? Or because of Dunn's modifications?

I leaned over the star-comp. Ken had pulled off, but not much. He was boxed in by two Federation ships.

There was a third ship. I put the star view on the screen and got a closeup. The third Federation ship was the Eagle. She was moving in close to us. Part of me, as usual, admired that pilot's skill and part of me felt a sick defeat.

The Federation had moved in on us and there wasn't a damned thing we could do about it. I thought about my nine-month battle to get the Federation to do something—anything about Ken and the Bella. Well, they did something, all right. They used me and they used our ships—

Beth came to my side. "What did you do?"

"Pulled in the connector." I met her disapproving gaze. How could she retain that autocratic manner in the face of all that had happened? "Silvernight and Garrison sent out the connector tube to hook up with the Gabby. They thought they were boarding her. I made sure they didn't."

"But why? Surely it wouldn't have hurt to help the Federation just this once."

"Wouldn't it?" I turned back to the star-comp. Beth obviously didn't know how the Federation operated. Why, with the evidence they had right here on this ship they'd tie her up for another six months, maybe even a year. But they wouldn't do that to the Gabby!

And the money in Illana Central—it might keep us afloat until this mess was all straightened out. If the

199

Federation let us keep any of it! But how could I explain all that to someone like Beth?

I rubbed my aching head. "You see, the FIS gives it to you with one hand but grabs it back with the other."

Beth's face went blank. She had no idea what I was talking about. I tried again. "Sure, we can gain the protection of the Federation's Service Arm on the inner routes, but then they turn around and tell us where we can and can't go! They pass laws and regulations that you never needed in the first place!"

Her expression didn't alter. For the first time I realized how very very far apart we really were. I could see it in her face. The Federation. The all-good, all-wise Father. I was blasphemous to decry the virtue that was Federation.

"Gil, we all have to live by rules and regulations."

"I'm sorry, Beth. I happen to believe that the laws we shouldn't break are the laws we make for ourselves."

"But then—you're saying that Garrison and the like—that they aren't wrong in what they tried to do."

"They were being true to what they believe. And they damned well didn't do anything I didn't expect."

"But how could we live if all of us made our own rules? I don't understand."

"I didn't say we all had to be pirates in order to express our deepest beliefs, Beth. Of course, we all have to take the consequences—" I glanced around the stripped down lounge. I'd done what I wanted and this was one of the consequences. And Ken—and my leg—everything and all for nothing. The lump of defeat grew in my throat.

I'd brought those extra drums of fuel halfway across the Cluster—also for nothing. Dunn would be terribly disappointed—

Fuel rods?

The Gabby—excitement knotted my stomach. Ken and I—

I took a deep breath and tried to steady my thoughts. Slow down, work it out!

I spun back to the star-comp. I had a chance, a slim chance! But I had to get back to the Gabby!

"What are you thinking, Gil?"

I smiled, and lied. "I've only decided to be grateful that we're all still alive."

Beth's answering smile contained the seeds of understanding. "No, there's something more. What are you planning?"

"Nothing. Honest." This was no time for her to read my mind! I turned my back to the star-comp and stared into its depths. There was the shuttle sent over from the Eagle. It approached on the cargo side aiming at Cargo Two.

Then Mike returned. By the set of his shoulders he was braced for another fight. A LEM was stuck in his belt, another was in his hand. "Silvernight and Garrison are back on board. They're in Cargo Two with the guards."

I remembered the two guards we'd tied up. Of course! Now it was plain why Mike hadn't released them. What lie had he told Garrison? That they were both unconscious? It wasn't important now, of course, but another inconsistency was cleared up! God, if I'd only been more questioning!

Mike opened the sleeper door on Reed's curious face and motioned him out. The shuttle docked. I could feel the vibration through the grid. "What happens now?"

"You'll go back to Illana with us." Mike touched his dark-stained shoulder.

"Oh?" Dead I might, but not while I was still breathing.

"Why does he have to go back, Mike? Don't you have all the evidence you need right here?"

Mike's jaw tightened grimly. "If I have anything to say about it he'll be charged with obstructing a Federation Officer in the line of duty, assault—"

"And taking the holy name of Federation in vain," I said.

Mike darkened, but before he could speak an officer in Service blue appeared in the galley passageway and saluted. "We're docked at Cargo Port Two, sir, ready to disembark the prisoners."

I held my breath. Would we be lumped with Silvernight, Garrison, Reed and the guards?

Mike nodded at Reed. "Take this one. There's six more back in Cargo Two."

"Yes sir," the officer grinned. "Saw them. Been busy, haven't you?" Then, looking at me, his grin faded. "This one too?"

"No. Trader Corbett and his wife will come with me."

I winked at Beth.

Suddenly Reed came to life. "Outrage! What do you mean? Where is everyone?"

Ungently the Federation officer shoved him toward the galley. We could hear him protesting all the way.

Suddenly restless I turned to the First Control and inspected the strange levers Silvernight had installed in the place of the 'Bella's normal control panel. I tried to keep my mind off what was coming.

"Stay away from those controls, Gil!"

Ignoring Mike, I studied Silvernight's fuel panel. I liked his core gauge. It was larger, more readable than Dunn's. I'd have to remember to tell Dunn—if I ever saw him again.

"Gil, damn it, I said—"

I turned on Mike. "Stop playing soldier, Pelonyi.

Obviously I'm not going anywhere, but no matter how damned hard you try, you'll not make me feel like a criminal!"

He flushed and shut his mouth.

The com-board chimed and because I was closest I flipped it on the big screen.

"Ah, Trader Corbett," Commander Sinclair appeared on the screen. "I trust you've left my First Officer intact."

Sinclair's smug smile made me angry all over again. Without answering I moved aside and let Mike have the com-board.

In their short conversation Sinclair ordered Mike to bring us aboard the Eagle as soon as possible. The other shuttle had already been dispatched to pick us up.

If only I could find some way to make that shuttle take me to the Gabby!

Then Sinclair added, "You might tell Trader Corbett that we've heard from Illana. His man there is out of danger."

Pete? I'd forgotten—a profound relief flooded me. "Mike, ask if they found out who—" But Sinclair was already gone. Well, a little was better than nothing. I smiled reassuringly at Beth.

She moved closer to my side. "I'm glad about Pete. Gil, how many weeks since we left Illana?"

So much had happened. I had to count it out. "Five and a half weeks. Why?"

"It seems longer."

I knew what she meant. Had that week on the beach ever happened? Would it ever happen again?

"I—" Pensively she glanced down at her hand on mine. "I wish we could start all over again."

I shrugged, trying to rid myself of the tension that was building between my shoulders. In a way I knew how she felt, but I wouldn't want to live through all this again. Especially now that I knew. I knew she could never be a trader's wife and I could never be anything but exactly what I was. Trader or stardrifter or whatever. Maybe it was meant that we should love—but not forever.

Suddenly she leaned closer and whispered. "Gil, whatever you have in mind, let me be a part of it."

I tightened my arm around her shoulder, but I wasn't much tempted. "No."

Stern-faced, Mike turned to us. "Time to go."

"Where?"

"Back to the Eagle."

I shrugged and held Beth closer. It might be my last chance. "Why not?"

Mike let us precede him down the passageway. My thoughts jumped ahead. To the shuttle. Would there be a guard? A pilot? How many?

"You know, Gil," Mike growled, "it's when you're the quietest I worry most about you."

I gave Beth another squeeze. "No need. I know when I'm beat."

And when I'm not.

Small worry lines appeared around Beth's eyes. Her jaw still held the red evidence of where she'd been hit. I felt my head where Mike had hit me, painful to the touch. And my leg ached. "What we need," I said to Beth, "is a nice quiet place to recuperate for a month or two."

"Like where?"

"Nowhere the Federation'll let us go, I can bet." I frowned. "Knowing them, they'll ship Ken and me to some rehabilitation colony for six months, impound the ships, make sure Corbett Trading Venture is good and dead, then turn us loose for lack of evidence. But I guess if worse comes to worst, I can always go back to work for Dunn.''

Beth half believed me. ''You wouldn't like that, would you?''

''No.''

''Damn it,'' said Mike, ''Federation won't do that and you know it!''

Beth ignored him. ''What about me, Gil?''—

''They'll slap you on the hand and send you home to mother.''

''But I'm your wife! I demand to go where you go!''

Mike's voice tightened. ''Don't listen to him, Beth. He doesn't know what—''

We entered the Cargo Two port area. A Service man appeared in the lock and we pushed our way past the clutter of gear toward him. He saw Mike and came to attention.

''And,'' I continued loudly enough so that Mike wouldn't miss a word, ''not only don't they care whether they ruin us, they'll leave our ship hanging here in space, unattended, with an overheated core, ready to blow apart. They couldn't care less about—''

Mike exploded. ''Gil, damn it, shut up!''

''But it's true, isn't it?''

He pointed me into the shuttle without answering.

The shuttle, regulation size, was bigger than a large hovercar, wider and with large open ports that made the screen superfluous. Its pilot had turned at the sound of Mike's angry voice. Mike stabbed a finger at him. ''Are you familiar with Class Four controls?''

''Yes sir, to a certain extent.''

''Then take charge of this trader's vessel.''

''Yes sir!'' He was young, and eager, and I wished him luck.

''Your main problem,'' I said, ''is that overheated core. You'll have to watch it. As soon as you have room, blow the vents—" I stopped in my tracks. "Mike, if that core goes critical, he won't be able to handle it by himself. He'll need help."

"Are you volunteering?"

I grinned. "Will you let me?"

"Get the hell up there and sit down!"

"Mike, listen, you've got an extra man here. Let him stay behind. If CTV loses the 'Bella now, it'll take everything we own to replace her and you know it. Everything," I added bitterly, "that the Federation leaves us, that is."

Mike's mouth tightened. He stared at me a long moment. "All right, you—soldier!" The man by the lock straightened. "Go with the Lieutenant. Do whatever you can to help."

The service man snapped us a salute that had a wry quality about it. Or maybe I read something into it that wasn't there. Relieved, anyhow, to be rid of him, I moved ahead of Mike toward the front of the shuttle and slumped down in a seat opposite Beth. Mike would have to handle the controls with his back to us. Would that make him uneasy? I hoped to God it did!

Leaving the 'Bella's side a moment later, Mike piloted the shuttle as if it were a space scooter. It reminded me of when we were cadets together. He'd always been a quicker study than me, but he'd never questioned the Federation's authority—and I hadn't accepted it even then. I'd made a very bad cadet!

Through the large front ports I saw the Gabby, still boxed in by the two big Class Sixes. A third Class Six angled out lower and to the left. We had to pass the Gabby to get to the Eagle. "I wonder," I said slowly, "if Ken's all right."

Beth glanced up. "Is he sick?" A frown furrowed her brow.

I nodded. "He's in pretty bad shape. Mike, has

your Federation quack gone over to take a look at him?"

"I suppose so."

"You suppose so! You mean you haven't sent a medic over there yet? Good God, Mike he could die!"

Mike glanced over his shoulder at me, exasperation in his eyes. "He's not that bad off."

"Bad enough." I noticed Mike had both hands on the control and was favoring his right shoulder. "Mike, let's pick Ken up and take him back to the Eagle with us. The sooner we get him help—"

Mike's stiff back exuded frustration, but he touched the view-com. I should've known he wouldn't do a thing like that on his own. Federation men don't even piss on their own. "Sir," he said when the Sinclair face reappeared, "Request permission to stop at the Gabby and pick up her pilot. He's also injured."

"All right, but hurry. I'm sending a pilot aboard the Gabby from the Hawk. He's on his way now."

"Yes sir. I left one aboard the 'Bella, too."

"Good, good. By the way, be careful when you get to the Gabby. I informed the elder Corbett he was to turn over control of his ship but he told me to go to hell. Might be a good idea to get him off as soon as possible."

Damned well and good for Ken!

Mike said to me, "Get Ken on the view-com. Tell him to stand by at the port lock. We don't have much time."

I moved to Mike's side and keyed in the Gabby's frequency. Ken appeared. Before he could speak, I said, "We're docking to pick you up."

"The hell you say! You and who?"

"Pelonyi. They're impounding the ships and taking us back to Illana."

"What for?"

"We got in their way."

"Gil, damn it—"

"Face it, Ken, what choice do we have? You know the FIS as well as I do."

"Better," he said. "I never did trust them."

I let anger touch my voice. "Anyway, get ready to be picked up. We'll be there in another couple of minutes."

A sardonic light touched Ken's eyes. "Whatever you say, kid. It's your show."

I grew tighter inside. Yeah, I got the praise and I got the—suddenly I laughed. The hell with Ken. Whatever he thought was his problem. I didn't have to keep on reacting the rest of my life every time he said something I didn't like! I flipped out the view-com and returned to a seat at Beth's side. I slumped down and sighed.

Beth gave me a worried look. "Is something wrong? Don't you feel good?"

"No," I said, "I don't. I'm tired. It's been the longest five and half weeks of my life." Looking at Mike's back, my mind raced. What could I use to distract him? What would be effective enough to—

Beth? Would she do it?

Never know until I asked.

I put my lips by her ear. Whispered, "Scream!"

Startled, she looked at me. Now? she mouthed.

I nodded.

Excitement touched her eyes. She smiled, then filled her lungs.

16

At a pitch to break glass, Beth's scream shattered the air. Mike froze but only for a second. Which was all I needed. He grabbed for the view-com but I chopped down on his shoulder right above the spreading stain of his wound. He gasped and fell sideways.

I grabbed for the LEM at his belt but he twisted away and I fell on top of him.

The LEM went off with no one in its path and I hit him—he lay still. I took the LEM from under his limp hand.

I was pushing myself up when an alarm sounded on the control panel. The harsh siren emitted tremendous urgency.

"What is it?" Beth asked.

"Don't know." I sat myself in Mike's seat and glanced across the panel. A red light flashed a warning in time with the siren. Air alarm! We were losing air! Panic touched me. What caused it? The LEM? Had it hit the unprotected side of the hull full force?

The Gabby loomed up in front of us. Using the manual stick, I swung the shuttle around to dock and we slammed alongside the Gabby's port. The Shuttle responded sluggishly to my hands. I came around again. This was no time for finesse! We bumped again, a solid smack that jarred my teeth and then the shuttle's docking mechanism took over.

Losing air the way we were, it'd be impossible to make a good seal. Speed now was our only saving grace. I'd intended to leave Mike, and Beth too, on the shuttle but now I knew I couldn't. I looked down at Mike. Much as I hated him, I couldn't leave him to die for lack of air. "Beth, help me drag him back to the port."

Nodding, Beth grabbed his legs.

The Gabby's lounge lock slid partly open. Ken stood there, a LEM in his hand. He stared at us. "God, kid, don't scare me like that. I thought you meant it!"

I grinned. "Serves you right. But quick, now. Get the port closed! The shuttle's losing air!"

With Beth's help we dragged Mike through and Ken slammed the port control. With laborious slowness, working against the shuttle's air loss, the port squeezed shut.

We dropped Mike on the nearest recliner. Ken looked down at him. "Is he dead?"

"No."

"Too bad." Then Ken noticed Beth. His jaw dropped. I made introductions, but Ken just stared.

"Ken!" He looked at me then and had the grace to be embarrassed. If I hadn't been in a hurry, I'd have enjoyed his expression. "How do we sit?" I moved through the Gabby's uncluttered interior to the controls. God, it was good to be home. I stared into the star-comp.

"Badly, kid. Can't move without hitting a Class Six." Ken followed me up front, started to slip into the First Control and then hesitated. A new note entered his voice I couldn't define. "You take her, kid. She doesn't handle nearly as well as the 'Bella."

It was a lie. She handled better. But suddenly ▶

understood and the excitement jumped in me. God, yes, I wanted the controls!

I spun around and dropped into First Control. The unit felt familiar to my hands. I checked the gauges, then the fuel.

Ken grinned and shook his head. "Damned stardrifter. I don't know what'll become of you." He dropped into Second Control and put the starfield on the big screen.

The shuttle was a darting light zigzagging away from us in obedience to the spurt of her escaping air. If we'd stayed with her, we'd be out of it by now.

Ken also watched the shuttle image. "What happened?"

While I ran down the other gauges I told him how we'd bested Mike. By the time I finished, his smile had turned grim.

Beth, having also listened, came to stand between us. "Is there anything I can do?"

"Yes," I said, "keep an eye on Mike and if he so much as bats an eye, use the LEM."

"Oh, Gil—" she sounded as though she never again wanted to touch another one of the lethal little weapons.

I smiled tightly. "No, Beth, I don't mean it. But if he starts to come around, let me know."

She nodded.

Ken faced me. I was sure he'd felt that undercurrent but there'd be time enough later, maybe, to fill him in. After all, we had a whole nine months to catch up on. I smiled and shook my head. "Later."

Ken turned in his control seat to look at Mike. "What about that Pelonyi? How do you figure him?"

"Just doing what he thought he had to do." And although I'd been mad enough to kill him, I couldn't stay mad. Not now. Excitement tightened my throat.

Touching the core control, I watched the core gauge rise to low normal and climbing. I glanced up at the screen. We were drifting. I checked the core again. The com-board chimed. Ken looked a question at me. I nodded.

Sinclair appeared on the viewscreen, his face tight with anger. "Corbett, what happened with that shuttle? Didn't it dock?"

Ken rubbed his head appearing puzzled. "No, Commander, it tried but couldn't make a seal. I think it was losing air. Are they all right? Is my brother all right?"

"Goddammit! We'll pick it up and find out. Watch your drift, there, Captain. You're coming in too close to the Hawk. We'll put a tractor beam on you if you can't hold her steady. The Hawk's shuttle will be there in less than five minutes."

"No need for the tractor beam. I've got control."

"See that you keep it, Captain!"

Sinclair's angry face disappeared from the screen and Ken gave me a crooked grin. "Pleasant chap, isn't he?"

I corrected the drift to throw us into a slow roll that brought us within meters of the Hawk's shiny side. The big Class Six moved outward to get out of our way and left a gap. A narrow sliver of space.

Beth, watching the screen, closed her eyes and shook her head. "It makes me dizzy."

"Once a landlubber, always a landlubber," I said. "Just don't get—"

Ken reached out a shaking hand, pointing. "There it is, kid. There's the hole!"

Big as life! I nodded and felt an adrenalin surge that made my skin tingle. I laughed at Beth. "Sit down, love, we're going for a ride you won't forget!"

She nodded and sank down into the nearest lounge

recliner.

I kicked the one-four pods in, and added the two-fives. Ken pulled his seat strap tight, reached over and tightened mine. I grinned again. The Gabby came out of her lazy roll with her nose pointed four degrees below the Eagle's belly. They didn't have enough ships to keep us boxed in! No way!

I shoved the drive bar full forward. "Here we go!"

The Eagle slipped beneath us before she knew what happened. And ahead of us was open space.

"Beautiful," murmured Ken. "Beautiful."

Our acceleration started at our pause speed of 1200 Ks. I watched the panel and felt the urgency like a hard knot in my throat. None of the ships gathered in the tight group had been stationary in space, only stationary compared to each other. The drift had been on a line toward the Juno Colonies. Now, at a slow 1200 Ks we were edging away toward the black velvet of deep space!

"They're coming around!" Ken's voice was wire tight.

"How many?" The speedic passed 1300, still climbing. The core heat read normal/cool. The fuel level, high/max. We hadn't even taken the top off coming from the Brothers!

Ken watched the screen with intense concentration. "Two—Eagle and Hawk, I think."

A soft groan came from behind us. Beth said, "Mike's coming to."

Damn it, why couldn't he have stayed out for an hour or ten?

Our speed hit 1700. High normal on the Big Six was 2000 Ks, or 2KK. But it'd take her longer than it took us because she had more weight to push. "Ken, what's the Six's top speed?"

"Three double K."

"How long before she hits it?"

"Don't know." He paused. "Core's medium normal and climbing."

My hands shook with excitement. We were doing it! We were running away from them!

Our rate of acceleration slowed. The heat in the core had jumped from normal and was climbing. *No—don't do it, Gabby. Don't burn up on us—*

"Kid—" Ken's voice was quiet, "the Sixes are closing." Suddenly the Gabby shuddered.

Ken turned, his face anguished. "Why the hell are they shooting at us?"

I twisted around. Mike was just sitting up and he held his hurt shoulder. "Mike, for God's sake, get on that view-com and tell them to stop shooting!"

Mike's face remained a hurting, angry mask. He shook his head.

The Gabby shuddered again.

I met Ken's look and knew how he felt. But if the Federation thought we'd stop now they had to be crazy.

I kicked in the final three-six pods and watched the speedic. We hit 2KK with the core approaching low maximum. My excitement mingled with a real fear for the Gabby's safety. I thought of Dunn and the work he'd done on these ships. The special pods—special monitoring equipment to record her performance—monitor! I reached over to throw the switch for the tapes to start their run, but Ken had beat me to it. When we had more time I'd have to remember to ask what happened to the 'Bella's tapes . . . .

Mike came slowly to his feet and I was conscious of him behind me using the star-comp table to steady himself.

The Gabby shuddered again, but gently, as though she'd been brushed with a kind hand.

214

We hit 2.5 KK, moved slowly to three and reached for four.

I watched Mike from the corner of my eye. What would he do? Would he keep fighting? Would he accept the situation? I half tensed, reaching for the LEM, but Mike's hand darted to the readout button on the star-comp. He stared. Just stared.

I turned back to the control panel. 5KK. "Mike," I said quietly, "get on the com before the Eagle's out of range and tell Sinclair we'll meet him on Illana in less than two weeks' time."

"What guarantee does he have of that?" Mike growled.

"My word, Mike. That's the only guarantee he needs."

The speedic passed 6KKs reaching for seven. I said it out loud. I met Ken's awed gaze. Then I twisted as far as my belt would let me to look at Mike. The anger had fled from his face. Ken pointed at the view-com and Mike nodded. The core gauge leveled off at low/max. The speedic read 8.5 KKs!

I located Beth in the lounge recliner. She smiled but tears ran down her cheeks. Women! I'd never understand them!

I came back to Ken. "Open the shields."

He nodded. Slowly the great metallic shields slid back, leaving only the clear, lead panes between us and the view of deep space. Ahead and above us spread the glory and splendor that was the Galaxy. To our right and falling below our line of sight was Juno.

I thought of the Brothers. A sad little colony of humankind diminished by their limited imaginations and ambitions. And then I thought of the Federation. If it cost us every credit in Illana Central to pay the Federation's penalties, it was worth it. It *was* worth it.

I leaned back in the control seat and looked at the

stars. Suddenly and inexplicably I was at one with the Universe.

PAN
Birney Dibble

PRICE: $2.25 LB752
CATEGORY: Novel (Original)

Pan was the first of a totally new species—half-
man, half-beast—the result of a unique scientific
experiment. The conflict within him threatened
not only the success of the experiment, but Pan's
own life, and the life of the one person who cared.